Queen Fae

NYC Mecca Series Book 3

By: Leia Stone and Jaymin Eve

To our children, who have no idea of the crazy things their mothers dream up.

NYC
Mecca
Manhattan
Bronx
Queens
Staten
Island
Brooklyn
The Island

Chapter One

The funny thing about fae...

THE FIRE CRACKLED as embers shot toward the sky. Leaning back, I enjoyed the heat enveloping me as I sank into my soft chair. My clothes were still a bit damp from the downpour I'd run through, so it was nice to feel warm again. Still, I found myself snuggling further into my furs. Tonight the cold was bone deep; so far the Otherworld's weather was far more extreme than New York City. We were on our second and final night with the gnomes, and this was the third time I'd been caught in turbulent weather as I raced from my small hut to the general gathering area where they prepared and ate their meals.

The gnomes had retired to bed now, which meant it was just Kade, Nikoli, and me around the huge copper pit, only the roaring fire to keep us company. With one ear listening for any unwanted eavesdroppers, I turned to Kade: "We still haven't received word from Baladar. Do you think everything is okay? What if Selene attacks your people?"

That was why I was late. I'd forgotten to take the flower with me and had to duck back. I was trying to keep the magical bloom with me at all times so I wouldn't miss a communication from Earth.

Kade ran a hand through his thick dark hair, sending the unruly strands out in a few directions. He looked absolutely massive sitting by the fire, his furs giving his already giant size an extra boost.

"I think with the time difference between the Otherworld and Earth, they're probably only just realizing what happened. It'll be fine, Ari. I trust my people to keep us from war for as long as possible."

I nodded, but I was worried. I had tried to stop Kade from coming with me. He was the king of the bear shifters; he had responsibilities to them. But he had refused, and secretly I was really happy to have him here.

Kade then lifted me from my chair, depositing me in his lap, sending my heart off in a race of pitter patters. I forced myself to focus on what he was saying when all I really wanted was to wrap myself around him. "We leave at first light," he said in a reassuring voice. "We'll find Violet and then return home before Selene can do too much damage."

I let out a sigh, leaning in closer to him. "It's hard for me to sit and relax like this. I need to get out of here and save my best friend. Who knows what the Winter Court are doing to her?"

Dark expressions descended over both Kade and Nikoli's faces, which definitely looked odd on the pale magic born. But I understood it, he was close to Violet too. All of us worried about her.

Nikoli leaned forward in his chair. "At least our time here has not been a waste. We have learned a lot from the gnomes. The information will definitely aid us in the coming days."

He made a very good point. The gnomes were an odd, earthy race. Roughhewn on the outside, with blunt speech and mannerisms, but not unlikable creatures. They lived simple lives, filled with hunting, gathering – a strong tight-knit community – and their dedicated metal weapon craft. They still hadn't completely warmed to us "highborn fae" as we were pretending to be, but were forthcoming enough with information.

We had learned that we were on the border of the fall and winter courts, in a stretch of lands that sounded like a rural outlier of the courts, which also explained the turbulent weather. Apparently the four courts controlled much of this world, or the moods of their leaders did at least. Not to mention the unstable mecca was making it worse.

We couldn't see it now in the dark, but there was a huge shadowy mountain off in the distance. This was apparently where the Winter Court's main city was. It was there we hoped to find Violet. We would set out at first light; the gnomes told us it would be a three-day trek unless we could buy some horses, which was pretty much impossible as we barely had anything left to trade.

"I just hope we have enough food to make the journey," I said, allowing myself to relax into the comforting heat of my mate. My body was on fire from being in his lap like this, our bond so newly formed that the need to touch Kade got stronger every day.

"Finn at least said that they were doing okay, and had their full rations left, which will help." Nikoli repeated the information I had given them yesterday, after being in contact with my familiar. Our other party of friends were in position now, waiting for our arrival tomorrow.

Staying with the gnomes had been the right decision to make, it had been very helpful in acclimatizing us to this world, but they were also getting plenty from the deal. They had all but cleared us out of food, except for what we kept as absolute minimum rations. Food was scarce here because of the dying mecca and the war between the summer and winter courts, which meant we had no chance of replacing that which we had traded.

For our food we got three exquisite, elf forged weapons, and two days' room and board. The elves were part of the Tuatha too, an ancient race who kept to themselves in the mountains and did not bother with the drama of the fae courts. Thankfully they made unbelievable swords. We were keeping the weapons back in the hut, and I was a little in love with mine. Every time I saw it I had to stop myself from pulling it out and examining the intricate detailing of the silver and gold handle, the way the blade narrowed to a perfect point, the sharpness that could cut though anything.

Another burst of coppery flames lit up the fire pit, and my eyes fluttered closed as Kade's hands settled on my shoulders and started massaging the tight muscles at the base of my neck.

"I love this freedom," I murmured to him, reopening my eyes and tilting my head back so I could see his dark, handsome features. "That we can be together in the open."

It was not something I was used to. Wolf and bear shifter couples were forbidden. Throw in that we were both royalty in our worlds ... we were screwed.

"I won't go back to hiding," Kade said, and I could hear the growl of his bear. "We are bonded mates. We will not hide that from the world."

He always says the most perfect things.

Our bond was the strongest thing I had ever felt, even when we were teenagers. I had fought as hard as I could to resist him, but in the end I couldn't. And it had cost me my crown. I wasn't worried, though, I was going to figure out how to have Kade and still be a just leader to my people. According to Baladar – who was old, wise, and definitely appeared to top the magic born power scale – bear and wolf royal couples had worked in the past, and it would again.

"We'll get her back, Ari," Kade said, sensing my gnawing worry that would not abate. I turned so I could face him, pretty much straddling his body. For a brief moment I got lost in his whiskey-colored eyes as I reached up and brushed my hand across the scruff on his chin, pulling his face to mine.

Lips barely a breath apart, I said, "Together we can do this. I have absolutely no doubts." If I'd learned anything in my time as queen, it was that Kade and I were stronger together.

His soft lips crushed mine, and as his scent and taste crashed through me, my head went light and my body tingly. I had no idea how he did this to me, but I was not complaining. When he finally pulled back I let out a contented sigh, which had a grin and dimple appearing on his face. Poor Nikoli had to put up with our constant physical contact when he had no one of his own. He was a good sport about it, even now he just sat quietly, eyes half closed, staring at the mesmerizing flames.

"I wish we could leave right now to get her," I murmured.

Kade nodded. "Me too. But this time has been essential for us. We now have weapons, furs, and knowledge. This might just be the thing which gives us the upper hand we were lacking before."

He was right, I knew that. We had ferreted out detailed information of the surrounding woods, people we might encounter, the best path to take. The gnomes had accepted our story that we were seeking jobs in the Winter Court, fleeing a scandal at the Summer Court.

All of us turned at the sound of wings. I sat up as Nix dropped down in front of us. Kade's majestic familiar had taken to flying around and hunting at night. She was not easily concealed, and we didn't want to draw attention to ourselves. When we travelled in the day, she'd either be flying low at our sides, or way up high to disguise her size.

Worries for tomorrow. Now it was time for bed.

I accepted Kade's hand up and helped put out the fire and gather our things. We made the small walk over to our one-bedroom cabin, thankful that the icy rain had ceased. When we reached the front door, Nix flew up to sleep on the roof. She would keep watch and alert Kade if anyone suspicious approached. Upon entering the cabin, Nikoli crashed onto the bedroll in front of the fire.

"See you at first light," the magic born said as he rubbed his eyes. "Oh, and we should wear our weapons. The gnomes told me there is no way we will make it to the Winter Court without running into trouble."

I nodded, my eyes resting on the three swords leaning against the wall, all beautiful and deadly. The gold scrollwork on mine made it look feminine, but the serrated tip gave it a lethal edge. Kade's blade was huge and thick. It had a base of branded steel and the tip had the slightest hook, making it an easy kill weapon. Nikoli's was plainer but still amazing, a shorter sword with a three-pronged tip.

We had really lucked out finding that gnome when we stepped through the portal to the Otherworld. We were armed in many ways.

"Goodnight," I told Nikoli, and made my way into the bedroom I had been sharing with Kade. My mate closed the door behind us, before crossing to sit on the edge of the bed and removing his boots.

I took off my boots too and then both of us crawled onto the bed. There was no point getting undressed, we would run in these clothes come morning, and we needed the furs to stay warm. It didn't matter to me though, just being able to sleep in his arms was enough for me today.

"Can you believe this world has existed parallel to Earth this entire time, without our knowledge?" I said, snuggling closer to his warmth and the hard muscles of his chest. His smell enveloped me as he tightened his hold.

"It seems there is a lot we don't know." His tone was dripping with anger. My mate didn't like to be kept in the dark about things.

Mate.

A fairytale concept, but it was a bond I already couldn't live without. From the moment our connection kicked in, we could sense each other's emotions and feelings, and even speak mentally if we needed, the same way we did with our familiars. I was still perfecting the mental-speak, but it was definitely nice to have it, especially in this place where certain things shouldn't be said aloud.

I could feel the heaviness of sleep pulling on me as I drifted off. I fatigued faster here; the lack of mecca was definitely hurting us. Luckily shifters were resilient. Still, the longer we stayed the worse it would become.

Darkness dragged me under, but instead of disappearing into the land of slumber, I realized part of my mind was still coherent, like I was in a sort of half-awake, half asleep state. Drifting in this groggy place, I heard Violet's voice:

"Arianna," she whispered behind me, and in my dream I spun around. My surroundings became clear then. We were deep in a forest of thick trees. This definitely wasn't a normal dream. I could still sense my body lying on Kade's chest, but part of me was not in that room any longer.

"Violet!" I rushed to my best friend to pull her into a hug, but she put her arms out to stop me.

"Don't touch me!" she shrieked, her face crumpling. I skidded to a halt a few feet from her.

Now that I was closer, it was clear Violet did not look well. Bruises and welts marked her face; she was paler than usual, which was saying something with her pigmentless skin, and she was very thin.

"Violet, we're in the Otherworld. I'm coming for you, hold on." I was freaking out seeing her look so sickly. We should not have spent two nights with the gnomes. She was running out of time. "Where are you? What are they doing to you?

She swallowed, holding out a shaky hand to calm me. "I'm okay. It's just ... they have most of my magic bound. It's painful but ... I'm okay."

"How are you projecting in my dreams if your magic is bound?"

Her face crumbled for a moment before she straightened again. "They weren't able to bind all of my energy. I tucked a small part away ... a hidden pocket of mecca they can't touch. It's how I've come into your dream ... but it takes a lot out of me. I don't have much time."

"Tell me what to do. Where are you? How many people are guarding you? What's the best way in?" I rambled on, trying to get as much information out of her as I could before she had to go.

Violet bit her lip and a tear drifted down her cheek, "Ari, that's not what I need to tell you. There's something more important you need to know."

My stomach sank. What could be more important than saving her?

Violet pressed on. "They took me for a reason. There's this small glass case here. It's filled with so much magic I can barely stand to be near it for more than five minutes. They told me they will unbind my powers if I can release the magic inside of the glass case and transfer it to Isalinda, the Winter Court queen."

I frowned. "That sounds like an awful idea … but if they will let you go afterwards, then do it!"

Violet looked even sicker, her face pinched in pain. "I can't. I mean … I might possibly be able to release it … but I won't."

I stepped closer. "Why? Do whatever you have to in order to get out of there, Violet! Do you understand me?" My panic was taking over. She was barely able to stand straight now.

Violet shook her head. "No, Ari. I can't. The jar flashes with scenes of your life. Your magical essence is in there. The moment I saw, touched, smelled, and felt it … I knew it was yours. Arianna, someone's been lying to you. Not all is as it seems. Your mother … has lied. I think your father is a fae."

The shock of her revelation hit me so hard my body was ripped from the dream state and I woke up panting. Kade was immediately alert, his hands tightening on me as he pulled me closer. I blinked a few times as droplets of liquid fell into my eyes; my whole body was covered in a thin sheen of sweat. As I met Kade's dark gaze, my breathing stuttered. Could Violet be right? Holy shifter gods, what had my mother done?

"Arianna!" The deep tones cut through my disorientation, and I realized Kade had been calling my name for some time. He growled then, before turning to yell for Nikoli.

I dropped my hand onto his chest, which had his eyes right back on me. "What happened? Are you okay?"

I nodded and shook my head at the same time, trying to figure out how to answer. "Violet just appeared to me in my dream. She's hurt – they're hurting her."

Kade's grip got tighter, before he gentled his hands again. "Did you tell her we're on our way? Did you tell her to hold on?"

"Yes, I told her." I wiped my clammy hands on the rough bed coverings. "She was barely listening to me. It took all of her energy to get through to me. She wanted me to know that the Winter Court have a magic-filled glass container there. They took Violet so she could free the energy and transfer it into the dark queen."

Nikoli was in the doorway now, listening in, his white features looking pinched and stressed. Kade and the magic born remained silent, letting me finish. "I told her to do it, do whatever it took to get out of there, but she said..." I licked my lips, searching for moisture. "She said the energy is mine. She made it seem like it was fae energy. Violet must be the only one who can figure out how to release it or they wouldn't be asking her."

Nikoli took a few steps further into the room. "Violet is bonded to you. Not only is she your best friend, she's also your palace magic born. She knows your energy better than anybody. The same way I am with Kade – we too were childhood friends. This might explain why they needed Violet to control that energy."

Kade exploded up off the bed, his body huge as the bear tried to force his shift. "How and why in the hell do the fae have your energy, Ari? Actually … how in the hell do you have fae energy to start with?"

I rose to my knees, my hands balled into fists in front of me as I tried not to panic. "I don't know. Violet's last words were that she thinks my father was a full Tuatha de Danann. A fae. That someone has stripped me of my powers and bound them to this glass container."

The room fell silent. Kade's body was still extra-giant and quivering, but he was keeping his bear contained. Finally Nikoli said: "I've cast a cloaking spell. It will last a short time to hide our words. This is not information that should be heard by others. We should be careful in speaking of this from now on."

Kade strode closer to his friend. "Should we be taking Arianna to the court? They might have taken Violet for this specific reason, but they still wanted Ari for something too. More than once now they've tried to pull her into the Otherworld. Now that we know she's possibly full fae … well, the danger seems too great."

I growled, low, trying to keep my burst of anger contained. "Standing right here, mate. I can make these decisions for myself."

Don't even try to over-protect me right now, I said internally through our bond. *Violet's information changes nothing in our plans. I will still be getting her back, only this time I'll be getting my powers back too.*

Because if some creepy-ass fae had my essence or whatever, locked up in their castle, there was no way in hell I was leaving without it.

I barely slept for the rest of the night. If I was lucky I got two hours in between my multiple freakouts. Poor Violet, she was suffering, and that had my wolf tense and my human side devastated. But I refused to allow either of us to fall apart. There were too many things we needed to deal with.

Like the fact I might be a fae? A full-blown fae? I was still trying to figure out how it was even possible. What the hell was my mother thinking?

She said she had chosen my father for breeding purposes, but she failed to mention he was a fae.

My frazzled mind continued to mull over the pieces of my life, trying to figure out how it could be possible. I was thankful when the first light of day hit. Both Kade and I sat up immediately. He had not slept any better than me, but at least for once neither of us were alone in our worries.

It took us only moments to gather our things and set off, with no more than a brief farewell to our small-statured friends. The gnomes spread out in a group, their faces serious as we walked away. I knew most of them thought we would meet our death in the harsh winter lands. I'd been underestimated before though, and I would be doing everything in my control to make sure no one died in the Otherworld.

Heading east, we moved toward the campgrounds where my dominants Monica, Victor, and Blaine were waiting. Finn, who was still with them, had sent me detailed directions through our bond.

My elven sword was strapped in its leather sheath on my hip, and my hiking backpack was stuffed with more furs, what was left of our rations, my small bedroll, and a makeshift tent.

Nikoli moved into my line of sight and his appearance took me by surprise again. I wondered how long it would take for me to get used to it. The last piece of advice the gnomes had given us was for the magic born to disguise his looks. His pale skin and white hair would stand out and attract trouble. Apparently the pale magic born were uncommon here. So now Nikoli had black hair, thick bushy eyebrows, caramel skin, and dark eyes. He said it would drain a lot of his magic to keep up this appearance, but once we were alone in our campsite or tent he could drop the illusion and take a magical rest. If we ran into any trouble that required us to fight, he'd have to drop the illusion then too. He wouldn't be able to do both. Hopefully that didn't happen before we met up with our friends.

As we walked, I took a moment to really enjoy the lands we traveled through. I had spent my entire life in a huge city, one I loved more than anything, but being in nature like this ... it was freeing. There had been a few villages off in the distance, but for the most part it was wide open plains, pockets of forest, and clear skies above. No skyscrapers. No cement. Nothing artificial or fake. The air smelled and tasted sweet, the plants and animals we encountered looked content, and my wolf was basically growling inside of me, wanting to go out and frolic in the wilderness.

Despite the mecca loss here, it was still beautiful, which gave me this craving to see this world when it was at its best, filled with energy and beauty.

"Do you feel connected to this land, somehow?" I asked the guys when we all paused for a brief break. "Like you've been here before? Or ... like your soul is freer here?"

Dammit. Maybe I am fae? Or crazy.

I was definitely a shifter. I couldn't be full fae. Right? At most I was three-quarters fae ... which was still bad enough. Ugh, I couldn't think about this right now.

Kade answered me first. "My bear finds this world calming, as nature has always been for me. I live in the city from necessity, not by choice."

This was something I had always known about Kade. There was a reason I'd found him in the forest when we were fifteen, and then again in his garden during the Summit. He was an outdoorsy type of shifter, and I loved that wildness he wore across his skin.

"The mecca energy feels pure here," Nikoli said, "even with the imbalance. When their energy returns, I can sense it would be much easier for me to wield power in the Otherworld."

So it seemed that all shifters felt the affinity of power here, maybe because all of us were part fae. Or maybe the Earth side was corrupted ... not as pure. It was confusing and worrying, but there was no time to dwell, we had to reach our friends before nightfall.

Everything okay with you all? It was harder to project my thoughts to Finn over distances – required more energy – so we didn't talk much.

We are still safe, waiting for you. I miss you, Ari. Hurry!

Miss you too.

I let the energy required for our mental link dispel, then jumped to my feet. Our rest was over, it was time to move. My urgency to be with Finn increased every time we connected. I couldn't wait any longer.

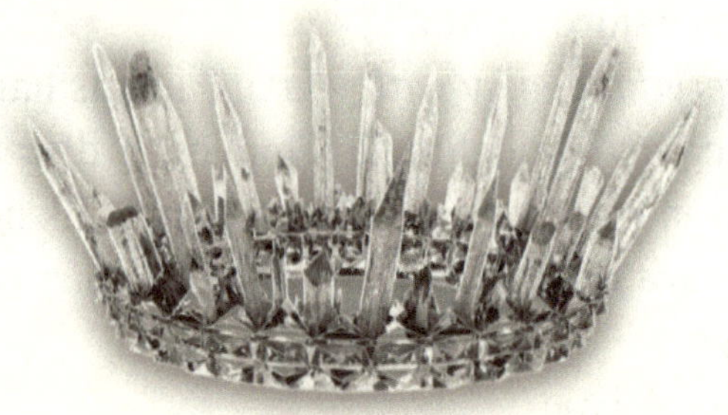

Chapter Two

The road to Winter is paved in souls.

WE HAD BEEN walking a few hours when we broke through a thick cropping of trees and the travelers' camp came into view. Kade sent Nix high into the sky so she wouldn't add to the unwanted attention we were going to draw no matter what. I recognized this sort of setup. Travelers would come and go, but the regulars would always pay close attention to any strangers. It was a survival skill, honed through experience.

There must have been fifty or more tents, with all types of fae creatures milling about. I tried to school my expression at what I was seeing, when in reality all I wanted to do was stare wide-eyed and ask them lots of questions. There were so many different beings: gnomes, ogres, highborn fae. There were also plenty of fae I didn't even have a name for. A group of tall, skeletally thin fairies caught my eye. They were hovering a few inches off the ground, gossamer wings flitting about.

Well, that's not something you see every day, Kade said into my mind, and I had to hide my grin. Yep, this was amazing, almost like stepping into a fairy tale.

Finn's energy burst through my mind. *I sense you. We're by the weeping willow on the water's edge.*

"Follow me," I said to Kade and Nikoli.

I followed a small path that led in the direction of my familiar's energy. Many eyes followed us, lingering extra-long on our weapons. We were intriguing them, which was never a good thing in a world like this. I kept my head lowered, making sure my hair covered my ears, as we made our way toward the giant weeping willow tree that kissed the edge of a small pond.

There were three tents erected in this small space, and coming out of the closest one was my giant white familiar. I wanted to run to him and throw my arms around him, to hold him tightly and renew our bond through touch, but that might attract even more attention, so I refrained.

I froze on the spot, just staring, drinking in the sight of his majestic beauty. He had a harness on, with saddlebags loaded with supplies so he looked like a work animal and not a familiar. Knowing I had to move closer, I allowed my leg to brush up against him, both of us enjoying the brief closeness. Blaine stepped around the corner then; he'd been somewhere behind the tents. As our eyes met, my best friend gave me a wry smile.

He was wearing a knitted cap, pulled over his very human ears. "Greetings, My Lady. May I be of service?"

I wasn't sure what game they wanted me to play here, so I waited for Finn to clue me in.

This camp is crawling with Winter spies that hear all and sell the information for a price. We said we're hired traveling muscle for those with money. We protect valuables from raiders and carry bags and such.

Okay, then. I addressed Blaine formally. "My companions and I seek your services in traveling to the Winter Court to find work."

Blaine nodded, his genial yet professional expression never faltering. "That can be arranged ... for the right price. When would you like to leave?"

Finn's explanation, and the fact that this campsite was so packed with people, was starting to make me very nervous.

"Immediately." I used my queen voice, slightly cold and forceful.

Kade stepped in beside me and introduced himself to Blaine, shaking hands. The entire charade was going very well at this stage, but I would feel a lot better when we were on our way.

Blaine nodded and looked back at Victor and Monica, who had been pulling clothes off a drying line they had attached to a tree. "Pack up! We've got a job."

Blaine took my backpack, Kade's and Nikoli's as well, and strapped them onto Finn. I knew my familiar could easily carry over a hundred pounds for hours without tiring, but it still pained me to see him this way. But this ruse was a good one; it would make it believable so we could travel together. Monica, Victor, and Blaine's clothes were dirtied and torn. They must have done that as a part of their lowly servant disguise. Whereas Kade, Nikoli, and myself were wearing pristine clothing with expensive furs and weapons. This would fit well with our traveling story.

I heard crunching gravel and then felt a strong energy at my back. I spun round just as the fae addressed me. "You'd have to be crazy to travel to the Winter Court in a time like this. The land is nearly impassable, and there's no work or food there." It was another highborn. He had bright copper hair, fair skin, and pointy ears. I don't know how but I just knew he was a Fall Court fae. He smelled of cinnamon and oranges, and didn't seem malicious. At least not yet.

Kade had been crouched, tying up the furs covering his shoes. He stood to his full height and looked down on the Fall Court fae. "We have jobs waiting for us there, and will make the trek just fine." His tone was light but there was a subtle threat. He wanted this fae to know he was interfering in our business and he'd better step back immediately.

The fae wrinkled his brow and inhaled through his nose, looking confused and intrigued. "Right, safe travels." He turned his back to us and walked off, and I noticed more than one creature was again eyeing our group.

Clearly the Winter Court was not a popular place to visit, and those who wanted to be there were considered evil or something.

He must smell the beast within us, Kade surmised.

It was probably our scents more than anything that had the fae here confused.

"We're ready, My Lady," Blaine said, bringing my attention back to the group. Monica, Victor, and Finn were saddled down with all of our gear, and definitely looked ready to head out. I felt awful for treating them as the hired help, but I loved that we could travel together. This was the safest way for us to move through these lands, so if they had to pretend to be below us for a short time, I knew they would have no problem with it. I would have done the same thing had it been reversed. This trip was about survival. Pride was not a luxury any of us could afford.

We left the travelers' camp without fuss, but I knew word would spread. We had created a stir, looking foreign, with a huge wolf familiar disguised poorly as a traveling servant animal. Thank the shifter gods Nix was barely visible in the dull skies above us. There would have been no way to hide two familiars. My dominants were quiet as we left, each of them falling back a little to walk behind us. When we were a few hundred yards from the camp, I pulled the small map from my backpack, one that had been amended slightly from the gnomes.

Kade glanced over my shoulder, Blaine coming in from the left to look also. My friend nodded a few times as he leaned in to see better. His finger came out to rest against the map. "We got those changes too," he said. "There are a few more villages, and some terrain we were warned against on this current path." He traced his fingers along the path, stopping about halfway between two large mountains. "I know we planned to take the trail through this range. It's definitely the quickest, but apparently is also a real target for bandits."

The gnomes hadn't told us that. I exchanged a glance with Kade. His eyes were very dark. "How much time would it add to our journey to go around it?" I finally asked, turning back to Blaine.

He hesitated a moment. "Two days, minimum. You have to cut around this mountain." His finger shifted on the map. "Go through the forest here, which is huge, before coming out on the other side. There is a steep drop on the other side, so this is the only way around the range."

Sucking in deeply, I forced my hands to steady on the paper. "We don't have that much time. We've already wasted two days here gathering intel. Violet contacted me. She's not doing well. We're going to have to risk the bandits."

The thought of risking my people made me want to throw up, or at minimum throw a punch or two, but two days extra travel time, or more, was not possible. We were just going to have to hope we made it through undetected.

No one argued with me, so I quickly folded the paper again and put it into my pack, right beside the flower from Baladar. *Come on, Baladar, call me!* I had tried to use the flower to speak with him many times, but either I had no idea how to do it, or the powerful magic born was not around to answer. I couldn't even consider the possibility that war had broken out in the time we'd been gone from Earth, that my friends or family might be dying and we had no idea.

They'll be fine, Ari. They are strong and sure fighters. This is not your fault – you don't need to shoulder the burden of everything on your own.

Having Finn back with me had a sense of calm and safety flowing through my body. As we started to walk again, I filled him in on what Violet had said in the dream about me possibly having a fae essence that had been stolen from me, an essence that would mean my father was from the Otherworld and that ... I was more fae than shifter.

What about Winnie? he said after I finished. *Do you think she is the same?*

My heart clenched at the thought of my little sister. She was well protected in Kade's royal home, but I hated that I had to leave her behind. I let Finn's question ponder in my mind, rolling it over and over. Finally I had to say:

I don't think she's the same as me. Mother loved her dearly, even though she never got to meet her outside of the womb. Me, on the other hand, she always had a hard time bonding with. It makes more sense if I have a fae father, and Winnie's was shifter. Maybe Mother was raped? Maybe she was tricked or coerced. Something which meant she could never love me the way she did her second born.

Kade's presence lingered on the edge of our conversation, using our bond to listen in. I was okay with that. He had not hidden himself and I could have blocked him out if I wanted to.

He spoke then: *Fae father or not, that changes nothing about you, Ari. You're strong and beautiful, wise and kind. You were a leader for a brief time and already garnered the love and support of your people. Your mother was the one with the problem, not you.*

His unwavering love and support was like a rush of heat that coated my skin and seeped into my soul. It was so much more than I'd ever expected I would experience from a man. Wolves rarely mated for love, and heirs never did. The best I hoped for as a queen heir was that I would be fond of the partner chosen for me, and instead the fates had blessed me. I got a bonded mate, and I would not turn my back on this for anything in the world – worlds. A change was coming in the shifter boroughs, and it was going to rock them to their core. Wolves and bears were never supposed to be separated, and I was going to bring them back together.

After we survived this little journey of course.

The path from the traveler's settlement was a fairly flat and easy hike. We walked for a few hours, stopped for a snack, and then continued on our way. The closer we got to the Winter Court's main city, the more the foliage around us changed. Gone were the burnt orange leaves of fall trees, and in their place were the gnarled sticklike branches of winter. With this change came a chill in the air that was beyond anything I'd felt before. It even cut through my thick furs.

Nikoli paused, turning his face upwards. "I sense trouble," he said, his eyes fluttering closed as he perceived things the rest of us couldn't.

Our group didn't move. None of us spoke as we waited. I tried to tap into the mecca energy inside, tried to sense what Nikoli was perceiving, but all I felt was the icy and insidious air as it slapped at my body.

Monica, Blaine, and Victor made the first move, falling into battle formation around me. Kade remained close to my side, Finn before us. No doubt dangers were everywhere here, even if I couldn't see them, so it made sense for me to unsheath my weapon. It would save me seconds if we were attacked. I would never forget how quickly that fae assassin in Kade's garden had killed so many of our guards.

A whistle cut through the air then, and an arrow burst out from the trees, heading right for Kade. My mind immediately flashed back to the last arrow from the Otherworld that had hit Kade. It had been laced with a fast-acting poison, and only Violet's magical expertise had saved him – Violet who was not with us right now.

Before I could panic, Kade twisted to the side and the arrow whizzed right past him to land in the ground behind us. In unison then, all of us lowered our stances into positions suited for defense and attack. Mecca crackled in the air as Nikoli dropped his illusion and threw up a magical shield. It had a slight purple haze and fell in a dome around our tight group. A few more arrows shot out. I focused on their arc – behind the safety of our shield I was able to calm my mind and follow their trajectory back to the shooter – to a pocket of forest to the right side of our group. The trees were almost bare of leaves, but we were too far away to determine how many attackers were waiting for us.

More arrows hit the shield, falling harmlessly to the rough ground. Movement drew my attention and I saw two fae, partially hidden behind some thick trees. Both were dressed in black robes, with weird chest and arm plates, like armor draped over a robe. One was tall and looked semi-human, the other had a thicker hunched-over shape, and something about his whole aura was giving me the chills.

Blaine turned to me as he pulled out a small dagger. "If you all distract them, I'll attack from behind."

Even though I wanted to protest, I knew we couldn't just stay safely behind the shield for long. Nikoli would tire; he was already weakened by having to hold his physical illusion for part of the day, and this extra shielding was going to drain him completely. We had no choice, I had to trust in Blaine's skills.

"Be safe," was all I said. I wanted to call out again as my friend crouched and rolled out of the protective shield, but I was afraid to distract him, or draw the attackers' attention right to him. Blaine moved quickly, ducking behind a tree, taking cover. I lost sight of him after that but knew he was going to work his way around, hiding amongst the trees until he was in a position to attack them from behind. Now it was time to keep the attackers' attention firmly on our group.

Monica stepped closer to the front of the dome, loading an arrow of her own. I was relieved that she had picked up a bow somewhere in the Otherworld. She was an excellent shot.

"I'm going to need you to drop the barrier for a second," she said over her shoulder. The barrier was designed to repel weapons. "Let me get a couple of shots off so they don't focus on Blaine."

Nikoli didn't reply, but the second Monica's arrow was nocked, the purple haze fell. Her hands moved so fast they were a blur, an example of shifter speed at its best, as she fired three shots in rapid succession, each moving straight and true toward the two fae. Both of the tall and creepy fae dived behind their trees, and Nikoli got the shield back up in a flash, protecting us again from retaliation.

I caught a glimpse of dark clothing high in the trees, which gave me a pretty good idea where Blaine was. He was slowly making his way from tree to tree, and looked to be getting pretty close to them. Monica readied her arrows again, and so far our plan seemed to be working. The fae were facing us, not noticing Blaine at all. I was just about to suggest we start moving closer to the attackers, but before I could speak, a branch cracked to the right of us.

We spun and my grip on the sword tightened as I stared at the beast only a few feet away. He must have been at least ten feet tall, with bony spikes along his shoulders, and thick, leathery skin that was the color of coal dust. *Holy crap!* He was definitely of the troll-giant fae family, and from what the treeling in Kade's yard had told me, their strength was unmatched.

The sound of cracking bones and tearing flesh beside me told me all I needed to know. Kade was going to shift and take this guy on.

One of the bandits yelled from their place behind the trees: "Give us your food, furs, and weapons ... and then you can go free!"

I wondered how many were hidden away there. We'd seen two, but there could have been any number further back.

None of us bothered to reply, we weren't parting with anything. I didn't plan on showing up to Violet half frozen and starving. We would need all our strength to rescue her.

Of course that still meant not getting beaten to death today.

Kade had fully shifted now – was he getting even faster? – his clothes in a pile at his mammoth bear feet. Nikoli dropped the shield just as Kade burst through to take on the giant troll creature. Finn bumped my leg and I quickly ripped the bag off his back, swinging one leg over him to ride. Most of my attention was on Kade. I was relieved to see him get in the first few hits. The creature was much slower than him; shifter speed was definitely an advantage. With a roar he barged the troll right into a tree, matching the troll in strength too, which was a relief.

The treeling had said a troll's strength was their biggest advantage. Their lack of brains canceled out most of that advantage though. Stupidity was something Kade could and would use against his opponent.

I was just about to help my mate when Blaine dived out of the trees near the bandits, drawing my full attention. He was going to be outnumbered. I couldn't leave him to take them on alone.

"Guard our stuff!" I called to Victor and Monica as I took off on Finn, holding my sword out, ready to cut these fae down. Blaine engaged in combat with the bow and arrow guy, which left me that weird hulking figure that had given me the creeps. As I got closer I could see he was still partially hidden behind a tree. What was he doing? He was just standing there like a weird peeping tom. Was he trying to scare me off? Or was he acting this way to draw me closer?

I was only a few yards from them when I heard Nix cry out from high above. Instinctively I knew something was wrong. I could feel it in my tight chest and throbbing head. Even though I had not been around her a lot, I sensed this wasn't her normal call. Unfortunately, from the ground there was nothing I could do to help her. I reassured myself with the knowledge that she was as strong and powerful as Finn. She could handle herself; hopefully that was enough.

I was almost at the tree and the creepy cloaked fae still wasn't moving. I kept my eyes locked on it, right up until a glint of metal caught my eye. Dropping my gaze, my heart froze and I shouted at Finn: "Stop!" My heels dug into his side as I hoped he would be able to stop in time. There was a round ring of glinting metal on the ground, hidden beneath some fallen leaves.

A trap!

Finn skidded to a stop, just managing to avoid the spikes, but before we could move again, another creature jumped out from behind the trees. *Holy mother of all things crazy ...* creature had been putting it nicely. The fae was completely inhuman, round, with three legs and a multitude of arms sticking out in all directions. It had mounds of glistening gray skin and teeth ... everywhere. Raising a bunch of its arms, he growled loudly, but didn't move from behind the trap. I brought my sword down hard onto the metal teeth and a huge circular, bear-style trap popped up from its hidden leaf bed and snapped closed. I just managed to pull my sword out in time. Swallowing hard, I was flooded with relief.

The sheer size and glinting sharpness of that device would have probably torn Finn in two.

That was close, my familiar said.

Yep, way too close. I was trying not to freak out about how close.

With a grunt the thing came for me, its gray skin crumpling as it moved. I was pretty sure I knew what it was now: an ogre. A seriously messed up one. Sucking in the chilled air, I tried to recall all the facts I'd learned about them. There was something the treeling had mentioned more than once, something they used in battle to give them an advantage, but for the life of me I couldn't remember what it was.

He was close now, and there was no more time to worry, only time to start slicing off pieces of gray grossness. It paused just before me and tipped his head back, and right then I remembered exactly what ogres could do. Acid fog. He roared, producing a green-tinged smoke from his mouth. Finn backed up as the smoke filled the area, but we weren't fast enough. Finn coughed first; a millisecond later the smoke hit me. Holding my breath didn't help, it seeped into my nose and eyes, burning like I had been pepper sprayed. My eyes and throat were scorched, and breathing got difficult, forcing me into a hacking cough, which loosened my hold on my weapon.

The ogre lunged for us both, taking Finn into a headlock and reaching for me with its other hands.

"Disperseio!" Nikoli called from behind me, and with a swirl of mecca the green mist was gone and I could breathe again. My eyes and throat still burned, but the shifter healing speed was already taking care of that.

Sucking in two huge gulps of air, I regained my grip on my weapon and sliced the blade up and across the ogre's neck – or in the vicinity of my best guess of where a neck would probably be. Luckily this was an elven made sword; I'd been told it could slice through almost anything, which was proven correct when it met with no resistance in the rocky skin. Black blood spurted out of the beast and he roared again, dropping his hold on Finn.

The ogre opened his mouth and I knew it was going to let loose with the acid fog, but before any mist emerged I swung at him and sliced through his open mouth. Using all my strength I forced my sword out the other side, completely removing the top of his head. The blackness of his oily blood spouted everywhere, and he hit the ground with a resounding thud.

Jumping off Finn, I quickly took stock of the battle. Creepy cloaked guy was gone; I could no longer sense his darkness. It looked like he had run. That would be a piece of luck we normally didn't get. Kade looked to be doing okay; he had the upper hand with the giant troll, pinning him against the tree and tearing into his body. Blaine, who had been joined by Monica at some point, had finished off the bow and arrow guy and they were now making their way over to me.

"You okay, Ari?" Blaine reached out and gripped my shoulders, his eyes scanning my body.

I leaned in closer and gave him a quick hug. "I'm perfectly fine, but we need to help Kade finish that giant. We've already spent too much time here."

My dominants nodded, then all of us hurried toward the battling giants. About halfway across the clearing, the sound of flapping wings closed in on us.

Nix! I had forgotten her weird cry before. I frantically searched the sky to make sure she was okay. Only it wasn't Nix flapping in my direction. Nope, it was some weird looking fae, almost like a fairy, but of the very dark variety. She swooped down holding her clawed hands out in front, giant black wings flapping behind her. The wings looked almost leathery, with a few shiny black feathers speckled across them. As she closed in I swung wildly with my sword, clipping her wing. With a high-pitched screech she rose up again, and seemed to be considering us as she hovered above.

Winged battle fae, Finn said to me. *They are related to the ercho. She might even serve the same master.*

Well, that was great news. *Just fabulous.*

Her pale skin was clawed up in places, and she had a few of Nix's feathers in her hair, which was long and dark, flowing out behind her. Her face was not quite human – the spacing between her features was too wide, eyes too small, nose hooked in an odd witch-like shape. She let out a blood-curdling screech; it was enough to have my eardrums aching and a headache forming.

Not battle fae … harpy, I sent to Finn. His growls burst free from his huge body, echoing over the area. The hairs on my body stood up, as they always did when he lost his cool and let the fierce beast inside take over. Harpies were a fae we had been warned about multiple times. They were the worst of their kind, battle-hungry and deadly, half woman and half bird.

My mind immediately flashed to Nix. Where was she? She'd cried out before and no one had even had the time to stop and check on her. I should have made more of an effort to find her. The only thing keeping me from losing my mind completely was Kade, still strong and battling without pause. If his familiar had fallen, he would not be so resilient.

A shadow in the sky caught my attention and my heart soared when I realized it was Nix. *Thank the mecca.* She was flying in a straight shot toward the harpy, who must have sensed the bird and was again heading for me, Blaine, and Monica. There was no way, even going supersonic speed, Nix was going to get here before the harpy hit us, so I braced myself, my sword held above me so I could swing at the bird-woman again.

It was an awkward position, Being attacked from above, and I was relieved that it looked like the harpy was focusing her beady eyes on me, which would allow Blaine and Monica to act as backup if I needed it. Three versus one gave me a fighting chance.

My dominants knew what to do. When the harpy was moments from reaching me, her screeches reverberating through my head, one of Monica's arrows whizzed over me and sank into its shoulder. She had waited for the perfect moment to let it loose, hitting her target in one of the softer, fleshy-looking parts.

The creature shrieked, her thick and massive wings pumping as she pulled up at the last moment, colliding with Nix who had still been descending. I took advantage of her distraction and jumped as high as I could, lashing out with my sword and slicing through her ankle.

More shrieking erupted from the harpy, and Nix launched herself around and completely encased the harpy's head in her talons. Blaine then took a running leap from the side, catching hold of her injured leg and pulling her to the ground. Nix held on for a second, so the harpy was almost pulled in two, before the familiar released her and Blaine slammed the fae to the forest floor.

Her wings spread out behind her, thick and bat-like, with serrated tips and a scattering of feathers. Blaine pinned her midsection just as she let out another harpy shriek. This time she was so close that I almost hit the ground from the sheer agony of her cry. In that second I would have done anything to stop that noise piercing through my skull.

I lashed out with mecca, aiming to cut off her vocal cords. My magic was wonky, but I did manage to lessen the sound, which gave me the time to regain my strength and drop my blade down on her body, cutting one of her wings off. Before she could screech again, Blaine drew his dagger across her throat to finish her off.

All of us waited for a moment; we had learned not to turn our back on any enemy until we saw their last breath. Then her chest was still ... she was dead. We jumped to our feet and I hurried over to Nix, who had just landed a few yards away. She was swaying, and I sensed that she'd been hurt badly.

"Nikoli!" I shouted, turning around. Kade roared louder than I'd ever heard him before, even when Violet had used the gold spell to heal his hand. He launched himself with strong and deadly force at the troll, and in a single movement grasped its head with both meaty paws and tore it clean off. All of our attackers were now dead, except for the one who had absconded. We just needed to make sure that Nix was going to be okay.

She has to be okay.

Kade was running toward us, his change back to human happening as he moved. I snatched up his pants, and as soon as Kade was no longer furry and bear-like, he pulled them on before dropping down beside his familiar. He scooped her massive body up into his arms, his muscles bunching as he held her close.

My throat got tight at the look in his eyes, part fury, part fear, all love.

"You did good. You're going to be okay," Kade said as I tried to take stock of her injuries. From the outside I could see her wing was bent and bleeding, but otherwise she looked okay. Of course, I had no idea what the harpy might have done to her in the air.

Nikoli was at his friend and king's side then, placing his hands on the eagle. A faint purple haze emanated from his palms, and within a few moments the bleeding had stopped. He ran his hands across the familiar, fixing up the wounds we couldn't see, until finally, looking pretty exhausted, he sank back onto his knees.

"She's going to be fine. Harpy got some poison into her, and her wing was pretty bad – she shouldn't fly for twenty-four hours – but otherwise she'll make a full recovery."

Kade nodded, still looking very ferocious and bear-like.

I surveyed the carnage around me. "Remember how I wanted to come here alone?" I said to no one in particular. I heard lots of laughter, some shaking of heads and smirks too.

"Yeah, not my smartest move. I'm glad you guys are here," I said as I grabbed my pack. My words were an understatement. There was no way to really convey how grateful I was to each and every one of them. They were my family.

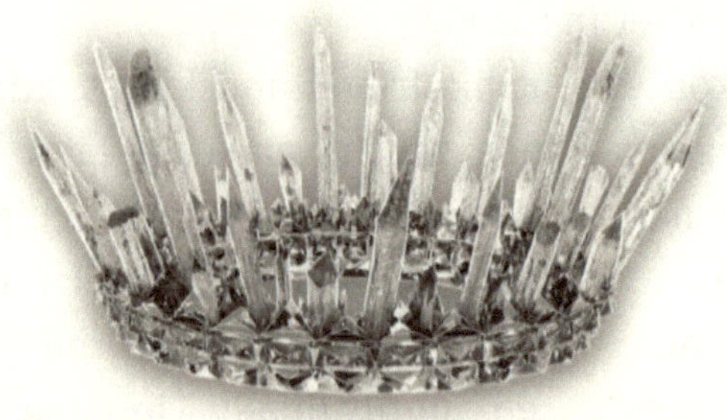

Chapter Three

Frozen feet. Frozen heart.

AFTER WE PATCHED ourselves up and gathered our things, we decided to walk a bit further and find someplace more secure to set up camp for the night. Even though the attack had been expected, and everyone had warned us we would not make it to the Winter Court unscathed, that didn't make it any less traumatic. Fighting creatures like that messes with your mind a little.

About forty minutes later we finally found a small area within the forest that had a mountain at our back, so we only had to keep an eye on two paths. I was tasked with making the fire as Kade and the boys pitched the tents. Monica was taking inventory of our things and doing the math on our food to see how much we would need to ration. Thinking about it made my stomach grumble; I was hungry, but so was everyone else here. I already knew what she was going to say: we didn't have enough to last the journey. Shifters needed more food than the average human; we were feeding ourselves and our beast inside. Not to mention that when we fought or shifted, as Kade had done, we burned through a lot of energy. Still, trading the food for weapons had already paid off. Our elven blades had served us very well in that last battle, and I'd rather be hungry than dead.

Nikoli, who had just ducked off into the bushes, pushed his way back into the clearing. He wasn't able to hold his illusion anymore tonight, he was completely drained of magic, so instead he wore his hood up and had rubbed some mud on his face and eyebrows as a disguise. He sat down on a log by the fire, which I just gotten going with a flint and a little accelerant. Thankfully Kade had thought to bring a fire starter kit, and even though it had been difficult finding dry timber to use – everything here had a dampness to it – the fire only took a little coaxing to really kick in.

I dropped down beside Nikoli, closer than was normally appropriate, but it was so damn cold, even with the fire. We needed pack warmth. Both of us were silent, watching the fire sparkle in the rapidly dimming light. It was never particularly bright in the Winter Court, and the nighttime here seemed to be darker than any I'd seen before.

As though he had to finally speak his thoughts, Nikoli shifted around to see me better, and said: "I hate to bring this up after we have just had a big setback but..." Cautious with his words, he paused. As an heir and queen, I was used to this. Despite my recent dethroning, most shifters still sensed the mecca within me, and even though I was not his queen, he'd still be hesitant to bring me news that would anger me.

"Speak freely," I said, offering him a small smile.

He nodded. "I respect that you have boldly taken this trip to save your friend, but it was hastily put together."

Okay ... that was fair. I nodded.

"I just want you to prepare for the fact that we may have to do some drastic things to get home once we reach Violet. As of now, we have no way of opening a portal home. I don't know how, and I'm pretty sure Violet doesn't either. Unless we find a mecca crystal for you to use, then ... well, drastic is pretty much where I'm at."

I stared back into the fire, letting out a sigh. He was right ... about all of it. I had hastily thrown this together, and we didn't have a way home right now. I had been so focused on getting Violet that I really had no plan A or B for getting us out of here.

"Tell me about this drastic," I finally said.

He nodded. "On the Island, there were two magic born who opened the portal on the hill the night they attacked. They didn't use their normal water portal, probably because we had many of our waterways spelled. I would guess it's much harder without a reflective surface to step between our worlds. Possibly, if we can find two magic born to help us ... or we might have to capture two of them and force their help..."

"Force them how?" I raised an eyebrow. Something told me beating the crap out of them wouldn't work. There was a reason the winter queen, Isalinda, had not managed to break Violet yet. Magic born were very strong of mind and will, otherwise they could never handle the power of the mecca.

Nikoli shrugged. "You leave that to Violet and me. Once we get inside the Winter Court I have a spell that will help me detect other magic born. Assuming this winter queen is as powerful as I think, she'll have a few magic born in the vicinity. We get Violet and then capture the winter magic born and flee through a portal they make for us."

"Easy as that, hey?"

He met my stare, and I knew both of us were pretty much expressionless. There wasn't much else we could do or say at this point. We were here now, and once we had Violet we would just have to hope that a path opened for us to make it back home.

Here's hoping that a little luck went our way at some point.

A warm body dropped down on my free and chilly side. Kade's scent swirled in the icy air and instantly I was warmer. He draped his arm over my shoulder and I was reminded of our last battle.

"How's Nix?" I asked.

"She's snuggled in the tent with Finn; he's sharing energy with her. Thankfully she's doing well, but tired." Kade sounded exhausted himself. Not only had he recently shifted to his bear form, but his familiar was injured. He needed food. Lots of food. Nix would be drawing energy from their bond, and without food both would be weakened.

The treeling had warned us to be very careful about what we ate here. Many things were poisonous or spelled. With the mecca imbalance, he believed anything edible would have to be scavenged. Which is why our rations were so important.

"Be right back," I said, jumping out from under of the warmth of Kade's arm. I made my way over to where Monica was still dividing up the food, her face pinched.

I dropped in beside her and lowered my voice. "How's it looking?"

She let out a long exhalation, teaming that with her pinched brow and rigid jaw. I knew it wasn't looking good. "This is each person's daily ration." She gestured to a small scrap of leather. I felt my face pinch up in a similar stressed look as I stared at the two tiny piles. Two meals per day – each pile had about ten cashews, three or four dried apricots, and one meat jerky piece. For a normal human that might be okay, but as a shifter we would be weak and worthless if this went on for too long.

I grabbed the leather piece and mixed the two piles. "Kade can have my share tonight. Don't tell him though."

She nodded. I grabbed up Kade's leather and quickly popped a cashew in my mouth before walking over to slide in beside him.

"Mmm, dinner is served," I said, handing him the leather. He took it and I chewed on my cashew. Kade would be able to see and smell that I was eating; he would never eat before knowing I was fed, and he would never knowingly take my share and leave me without. Never. But he needed it more than me.

Even with all my fake eating, the leather remained untouched in his huge, outstretched hand. "Where is yours?"

I patted my belly. "Wolfed it down while talking to Monica."

Wasn't even a total lie, I had definitely wolfed that cashew down. I was thankful that at the moment we were still being pretty mindful of each other's thoughts. I was doing all I could to keep our shields in place.

"I can feel your hunger," he said finally, holding out the leather. "Take my rations, I am fine."

Love swelled up within me until my chest felt like it would burst. I gently pushed his food toward him. "I'm not hungry, mate. You need it much more than me. Think about Nix."

Kade's gaze flicked to the tent where our familiars were recovering and I knew I had won this round. His meal disappeared in about twenty seconds then. He placed the leather on the ground beside him, and even though he didn't complain or act like he was hungry, I knew he was still starving.

As the others moved around the fire with their meager rations, Kade lifted his head and eyed our people. He wrapped his arm around me again so that I was pretty much in his lap when he said, "When we get out of here, I'm having a big fancy dinner at my house to celebrate. There will be mounds of food. Roasted lamb, duck and quail, scalloped cheese potatoes, and all the sides."

"And chocolate fondue!" Monica piped in and I smiled.

"Pretzel bread and cheesecake," I added.

"Bacon," Blaine said, pretty much drooling.

"So much bacon," Victor agreed, sounding much more like my old friend. The one he had been before he lost both of his brothers to Tuatha attacks. I knew Victor was irreparably damaged from these losses, that I'd never have the same fun loving, part-time chef, part-time jokester back. But I had some hope that we would all make it through this and come out the other side with some semblance of happiness.

I reached across and found his hand in the darkness, a memory springing to life in my mind. I let out a chuckle as I said, "Do you remember that night after we got drunk playing poker, and you decided to cook dinner for us." A grin was already across his face, he knew exactly what night I was talking about.

"Ben thought he'd lost one of his new little fire-cracker weapons inside my quiche."

Blaine let out a snort of laughter. "And he only bothered to remember after we all ate dinner."

There were a few more chuckles. We had all wondered for a few hours if one of us was about to blow up, but thankfully it had fallen into Ben's shoe when he took them off at the door.

There were so many memories like that for all of us. So many times together as a pack and family. In a blink of an eye everything had changed, making us all realize how fragile life really was.

"I miss cooking," Victor finally said, the crackling flames lighting up his handsome face. He was a bit more roughhewn than the other guys, but this gave him a rakish sort of look. "I just can't find the joy in it without Ben and Derek. I can't find the joy in anything."

He was an amazing cook, but it had been a long time since I tasted one of his crazy dishes. He liked to experiment with flavors. Sometimes it worked, other times it was a hilarious and messy disaster.

I squeezed his hand hard before crawling over my mate to fully wrap my arms around Victor. Outside of Blaine I had not hugged my dominants much, protocol and all that rubbish, but I was totally done with that now. Even if I were to be queen again, I would not want to hold myself back from them ever again.

"I wish they were here with us," I whispered, breathing in deeply as I fought tears. More arms were around us then and I could feel the energy of Monica and Blaine. My body was still across Kade's so his comforting presence was there also. His large hand splayed on my lower spine.

After many moments of comfort we pulled away. There were cleared throats and shiny eyes all round, but in some ways I felt a little lighter. And I thought my friends did also.

The silence was relaxing then as everyone ate their meagre rations. I sank into Kade, listening to the fire crackling and the frigid wind blowing through the trees. I was almost dozing off when a weird feeling came over me, a tingling of mecca, which had not happened much so far in the Otherworld.

Wide awake now, I looked around. I could swear there was a tiny voice coming from somewhere close to me.

I sat straighter. "Did you hear that?" I asked, trying to figure out what was going on. Was this another fae creature? I really wasn't up to battle number two today.

Something dawned on Nikoli's face then. "The flower!" he whisper yelled.

Oh! I scrambled to get my frozen hands out of my furs so I could search my inner breast pocket for the flower that linked me to Baladar. As I pulled it out, I was still astounded that it wasn't crushed, not even a single bruise on all the beautiful petals. Gotta love mecca energy.

I placed the flower to my ear, and even though I was expecting it, still jumped when I heard Baladar's voice. "My Queen? Are you there?" He sounded urgent. I pulled the flower from my ear and brought it to my lips.

"I'm here!" I said, and then brought it back to my ear as Kade leaned in closely.

"Oh, thank the gods. I don't have long to speak right now, there is much I'm doing here to keep war from erupting. I just wanted to let you know that help is arriving shortly."

My head whipped back so fast that I almost cracked Kade in the face.

"Help? Who? And what do you mean war?" I asked the flower.

Had he sent more people through to the Otherworld? *How?* Only Kade and I could open the portal.

Baladar said in a rush, "Selene has declared war on the bears. Provided false evidence that they were in cahoots with the fae. She wants all five boroughs, all that mecca power."

Kade's bear rumbled beside me as he gently pulled the flower in my hand to his lips. "My mother and Gerald ... are they aware? Are my people okay?"

Baladar snorted. "Your mother is preparing for battle. She tried to stop it, asking for a private meeting on neutral ground with Selene. Calista was there."

Oh no. That had to have been a disaster.

"Twenty seconds with that disgrace of a wolf queen and your mother slapped her across the face and then agreed to her terms of war. Each side has two days to remove children and pregnant women to the Island, which will remain neutral territory for the duration of the battle."

My stomach dropped. "Winnie..."

Baladar's reply was instant: "Already safe at Kade's Island home under fierce guard. I must go now. I just wanted you to know that help is coming."

The tingles of mecca disappeared in an instant and I knew he was gone.

What. The. Heck?

I sat back, my head buzzing. How could she? How could Selene break a peace that had held over a hundred years?

"I'll kill her," Kade said beside me.

I shook my head. "No. She's mine." My words were barely distinguishable from the growls ripping through my chest. My wolf was ready for blood.

Selene was already on my list of people to wipe from the Earth. Now she had just reached the top spot.

Despite my hunger, the cold, and a million other worries, I slept soundly that night, wrapped in Kade's arms – except when it was our turn to keep watch for attacks. His presence kept the horrible stuff at bay. Unfortunately, there was no way to hide in our tent forever, and all too soon morning dawned on the icy land.

As the first dull rays of light broke through to illuminate the tent, my eyes fluttered open and immediately my stomach started to rumble. One thing I was not great at was going without food. As a royal member of the packs, we always had the best of everything to eat. Still, this was not a huge sacrifice to make for Kade and Violet. I could go hungry for a few days. Surely.

My wolf whined but didn't let loose with growls, and since I was able to keep her contained inside, I knew she agreed with me about being able to do without food for our pack.

Kade had me spooned in against his body, our furs draped tightly around us. We were still fully dressed in case of battle, and also so we didn't freeze to death. Rolling over, I faced him; his arms tightened around me and I was hit with the full force of his bronze eyes. They were light for the most part, darkening to a rich whiskey close to the pupils, framed by dark, thick lashes. They were still the most beautiful eyes I'd ever seen; I could have stared into them for hours and never grow bored.

"Morning," I said, still amazed that he was here with me.

His lips descended onto mine and I fell into the kiss like a thirsty person to a glass of water, drinking him down, taking in everything that was Kade. My lips parted and his tongue slipped inside, stroking my own. His bear growled, chest rumbling.

"We really need some privacy," I murmured against him. Some of his growls turned to deep, echoing laughter as he pulled back to see me.

His hand brushed against the side of my face, pushing back some of my unruly white-blond hair. I kept it closely bound here so that it didn't draw attention, but I had to let it loose for sleep – it gave me a headache otherwise.

"Soon, Ari." He cupped my face. "Very soon we will have all the time in the world to wake up like this, and stay in bed for hours."

"I'll hold you to that, King Kade."

Some of his joviality fled at my use of his title, and I knew immediately what held his concern. "Gerald and your mother will know what to do," I murmured. "We lost many wolves during the battle on the Island, and Selene is a new queen. There's weakness in our boroughs – this is not going to be an easy battle for her. Not to mention the wolves will not like that she has declared war when they are still recovering from the last fight."

Selene probably wouldn't even see it, but she was making my job of getting the crown back that much easier with her irrational behavior. The wolves would not like it, and they would eventually rebel.

Kade relaxed a little. "I have every faith in my people. They'll not want this fight, but they will do everything they can to protect the dens and boroughs. It's just ... I should be there. I'm their king and without my energy they're weakened."

He was right, our leader held our boroughs together, and if there was any way for me to send him back, I would.

I'd never leave you, Ari! Never. That promise seemed so much stronger through our mental link.

Leaning over, I pressed my lips once more to his, before rolling across and jumping to my feet. "It will be an even fight. The young are safe on the Island. Let's just focus on getting Violet and then getting back home to stop this before it rages out of control."

Kade was on his feet in a whir of motion, moving with shifter speed. I had a moment of envy because I felt like an old woman today, low on energy and spirit.

We made short work of packing our things and pulling the tents down. The fire had burned out through the night; no one bothered to light it again, we were heading out as soon as we were packed up. Finn was close by my side and I found myself sinking my hands into his fur more often than normal. I needed the comfort, and besides Kade, Finn was the absolute best. Nix didn't move from the king's shoulder the entire time they were packing. I had no idea how Kade managed to do anything with a massive eagle on his body, but he never made it look like a burden.

Just before we were to set out, Monica held each of our rations out for us, and even though I wanted to pass mine to Kade again, he was watching me far too closely. I didn't fight, because I knew I needed to have some energy or I would run the very real risk of losing control of my wolf. Shifters were part animal, with lots of base instinct going on, and a hungry animal would do a lot to get food.

Finally we set out, just as the sun started rising in the dull sky. From my experience here so far, the warmth wouldn't be around for long, but it was nice while it lasted, giving us all a boost to our energy. I still had my furs on, but instead of them being just warm enough, I was actually cozy.

The land was changing as we traveled closer to the main village. I knew we were deep in winter territory now. It was still very natural, with lots of forest cover, but for the most part the plants were winter barren, no leaves or greenery, except for a few breeds that seemed to thrive and blossom under the frigid conditions. One especially was all around, giving these bright pops of red foliage against a wintery background.

So much beauty here. Made perfect sense when teamed with all the danger. In my world the most beautiful things were often the deadliest. Selene was a perfect example of that, although she added in a healthy dose of evil and crazy to her deadly.

When we reached a valley that passed between two massive mountains, their craggy peaks towering over us, Kade pulled his map free from his coat. "Looks like there'll be a small village on the other side of the pass. After that, there's nothing until we hit the main village and royal palace of the Winter Court."

Nikoli, who was still recovering from yesterday's attack, whispered a few words and his disguise was back in place. A little less complete than the one he had been using before, his skin was not as dark, hair not quite so different, but it was enough to hide him for a quick trip through a town.

We were silent as we made our way between the pass. The light grew dull as the mountains blocked out the natural illumination. It fell well below freezing, and I was once again shivering in my furs. Slipping my fingers deeper into my thick, lined pockets, I actually started daydreaming about the summer in the city – hot, humid days … ice-cream … walks through Central Park…

I missed my boroughs and my people. I missed being queen, even though it had been such a short time. And I especially missed Winnie. My little sister had better be okay when I got home or I would bring our entire world down in one crumbling heap.

In my musing daze I hadn't been paying attention to the outside world, which was a rookie mistake when traveling through dangerous lands. Lucky for me my mate was always on the ball. He yanked me out of the way as a huge boulder tumbled from above and almost squished me flat. As more tumbled down the cliff, all of us pressed ourselves to the wall.

I craned my neck to try and see what was happening high in the mountains. Was this a natural rockslide, or more sinister? We could have easily been killed; some of the boulders that had fallen on our group were as big as my torso. The timing alone had me thinking attack, but sometimes Mother Nature was just doing her thing.

Nix took off from Kade's shoulders with a loud, echoing squawk.

"Wait!" Kade's voice was stern as he tried to halt his familiar, but she was having none of his over-protectiveness. *You go, girl!* It hadn't quite been twenty-four hours since Nikoli had given her a flying ban, but she looked to be moving easily. She was probably dying to stretch her wings.

The valley was wide enough that she could flap her huge wings, ascending rapidly, zooming from side to side so as not to make an easy target. Rocks were still falling, most situated where we were standing, but also a few more up the path, which would make running very difficult. I leapt to the right when a huge boulder crashed close to my legs, before it bounced off the wall.

Nix screeched again, this time much duller. She sounded like she was way up the mountains.

Is she okay? I checked in with Kade and Finn, both of them able to communicate with her easily.

There are bandits in the mountains. Kade's mental voice was growly. *She said they have a full setup up there ... they must take out travelers and steal their possessions.*

Smart. If Kade hadn't sensed that first rock falling and yanked me out of the way, I would have been squashed, and then when my friends tried to help they all would have been too.

A shout rang through the valley and another object dropped from above. This time it wasn't a boulder, nope, it was some little green fae with leathery skin, pointy ears, and huge bulbous eyes. Well, they looked bulbous with him splattered across the rocky floor.

His death was followed by three more. Nix was cleaning up shop and she was taking no prisoners. "What are they?" Monica asked, poking her head out around Blaine so she could see better.

"I think goblins." Okay, that was a total guess. I didn't know every single creature who made up the inhabitants of this world, but the treeling had given me a solid overview. I knew goblins were green, and kinda evil, so it made sense.

After ten minutes, the rocks had stopped tumbling down and so had the goblins. Nix had brought down four of them; none of them were moving from where they had tumbled. Thankfully their skin seemed to be even tougher than leather, because there wasn't a whole bunch of blood or guts spilled everywhere. They remained intact. Flat and intact. Still pretty disturbing.

As soon as Nix made her way back down to rest on Kade, it was safe for us to set out again.

"Nix can have my beef jerky ration tonight," Blaine said with a grin.

Everyone chuckled, and Nix gave Blaine a head dip, her majestic and wise eyes unblinking.

Our laughter disappeared as we focused on getting out of Death Valley without further incident. I was really relieved to see the end closing in, and then we were out and winding our way down a long path. In the far distance I could see some gates and small buildings.

The village.

It took us a bit of time to finally make it down, but when we did I fell a little in love with the quaint township. The huts were modest and the village folk looked like a mixture of fae, but none of the crazy, giant ones. We kept our heads down and only nodded or gave a polite smile when necessary, not wanting to draw too much attention. I almost failed at remaining undetected when we passed a food cart. I had to physically restrain myself from begging them for a taste of the meat being butchered and prepared, before being tossed onto a skillet. The animal looked a bit like a rabbit – whatever it was, it smelled delicious.

Did we have anything else to trade? We didn't bring any modern jewelry, like watches, for fear of being recognized, and I wouldn't dare part with my furs. *Sweet shifter gods I was hungry.* It worried me that we might have to steal, because our rations were not going to last until we got to Violet. I had no doubt that to successfully rescue her, we would need our full strength. I hated the thought of stealing from people who looked like they didn't have much to give, but it was life and death for us, and I would find some way to pay them back.

Stopping in what looked like the town square or center of this village, we huddled together trying to decide if we should camp here for the night or pass right through. Everyone was tired and hungry, but we hadn't actually walked very far today. We would probably have to press on. I was just about to mention stealing some food before we left when I felt a tap at my back.

I spun quickly, my hand already closing around the hilt of my sword, ready for a confrontation. I stilled as I found a little boy before me. He stood no taller than my waist. On Earth, I would have put him at the age of eight. Here, I had no idea. His big brown eyes were locked onto my elven blade, wide and fearful. His pointy ears peeked up out of his matted mess of hair; he was covered head to toe in dirt. I immediately took my hand off the blade so as not to spook him further.

With a shake of his head, he took a deep breath, leaned into me, and whispered so low I could barely hear: "Arianna?" He seemed unsure.

What the actual freak? I'm sure my eyes went as wide now as his had been when staring at my blade. Kade, sensing my shock through our bond, stepped closer to me, ready to protect me if needed.

The boy was still waiting for an answer, so I nodded. Without another word he turned and ran, making his way down a nearby alley that passed between two of the taller huts. I swiveled so I could see Kade. His brows were raised with a what-the-hell-is-going-on-here look.

I shook my head. I had no answer. But this child knew my name. Which meant we should follow. Right?

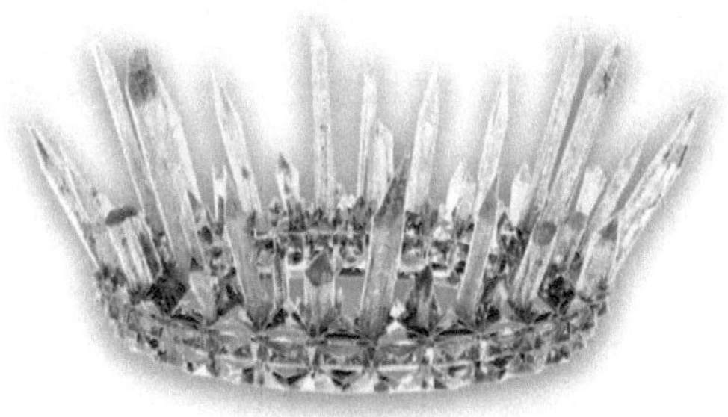

Chapter Four

Help is only a flower call away.

BEFORE I COULD move, the boy caught our attention again, reappearing close by and waving us on.

"No way," Kade said. His hand had not moved from his sword. "This is probably a trap. How does he know your name?"

I shrugged. "I have no idea, but Baladar did say help was coming ... maybe this is it. I'm willing to take the risk." Before anyone else could protest, I took off after the kid. Kade's groan followed me, along with the sounds of our people grabbing their stuff and hightailing it after me.

The boy took a left at the end of the alley, I kept a reasonable distance between us as I followed. I might be willing to take a risk, but I wasn't planning on being completely reckless. I kept him in sight, but left enough distance to give me warning of an ambush. Finn was at my side, his warmth comforting.

Turning another sharp corner, I paused at the same time as the boy. He slowed to a walk, crossing to one of the larger, more square style huts. He held the door open, waving us all inside. Kade's hand came out to stop me before I could cross and enter the building.

His bear-like focus went to the child. "Who sent you?" His words weren't cruel, but there was a sense of power behind them.

The young fae did not hesitate. He was clearly not worried about revealing any secrets. "Some lady sent me to lead you here. She is not from this court. She smells of warmth and flowers. Come on or I won't get my meal."

The boy disappeared inside. None of us moved for a moment. Inside was a complete unknown and it could definitely be a trap. Still, the smells of sunshine and flowers thing had me hoping it was a Summer Court fae.

Kade pulled his sword and strode toward the door, making sure he was first. Always the protector, it's what made him such an amazing mate and king.

I hurried up behind him, but before we could step through Finn blocked both of our paths.

Let me go first. They won't expect a familiar and may not attack. They'll think I'm a stray wolf.

Um, pretty sure they'll attack you even if they think you're a wolf. Food and fur is pretty valuable in this world.

Finn's rumbling bark of laughter echoed across my mind. *I'm hard to kill, Ari. Let me at least scout it out before all of you serve yourselves up into a trap.*

With a sigh, I nodded, relaying the plan to Kade. He didn't look any happier about Finn going in than I was, but he said nothing as he held the door open for him. It was agony letting my familiar go in first, but I had never and would never be the type to over-protect him to the point he had no rights or choices. He wasn't my pet. If he felt he could do this, then I would let him.

I raised to the balls of my feet, weapon in hand, just waiting for any sign of trouble. I'd be in there so fast, and whomever had hurt my friend had better hope they killed me. Otherwise I was going to destroy them. Close to my side Kade, Monica, Blaine, and Victor all had their swords at the ready.

Within moments of entering, Finn's presence in my mind relaxed. There was a sense of shock there, and also happiness, before he said: *Come in. It's safe.*

"It's safe," I said, stepping forward and pushing the door wide open.

On the inside, I realized this was the back entrance to an inn or tavern of some sort. I passed a bathroom door, then the kitchens, the smell of something tasty, maybe a stew, teased me and my wolf. Stepping into an open dining hall, I scanned the room for Finn, finding him near a back corner booth. And he was with someone I recognized. A smile broke out across my face. *Thank you, Baladar.* Dalia, the Summer Court fae I had met in Astoria Park, was sitting in a corner booth, another hooded fae at her side – who had their face well hidden beneath the shadows of the cloak.

Dalia stood as we approached her table, and gave me a nod before putting a fist across her chest and bowing low.

"Arianna, well met." Despite the formality of her gesture, she had only used my first name, her eyes darting around. No doubt she wouldn't want to call me Your Highness, for fear others would hear.

I gave her a warm smile. We were sorely in need of some assistance, so my joy in seeing her was genuine.

"Well met, Dalia," I said, before she gestured to the chairs around the long table she had chosen. More than large enough to accommodate us all.

We wasted no time taking our seats, and my stomach let out a massive rolling growl when a server approached us with a huge tray filled with steaming bowls of something delicious smelling.

"Thank you," Dalia said as she gave him a polished gold coin. Then she added a second shiny coin and waved toward the rest of us. "Room and board for the night as well."

The server bowed lightly and pocketed the coins. "I'll get the rooms ready."

Grabbing one of the bowls, I dropped it down to where Finn was resting beside my chair. He was just as hungry as the rest of us, and Kade took a bowl out for Nix, hiding on top of the building, keeping watch. The stew was not either of our familiars' favorite meals, but it would do in these circumstances.

Dalia's friend still hadn't said anything, but as soon as Kade was back at the table she lowered her hood and her very pale face came fully into view. *Magic born.*

When she finally did speak, it was quietly, her voice low and husky, tingling with energy. "You may speak freely. I have spelled this corner of the room."

Her words were like magic in themselves; mecca dripped from each syllable and I felt my own energy respond. I had been getting used to the loss of power in the Otherworld, the weakness of the mecca, but having a source like this at the table with me set off a ricochet of energy through my gut, reminding me of all we'd left behind.

The magic born sat forward in her seat, allowing more of the cloak to fall from her shoulders. She was a tiny thing, even though she was sitting. I would guess she didn't stand any taller than five feet. Her hair was white, but with a tinge of silver to it, like strands of the metal were woven through the long fat curls that tumbled over her shoulders. She had light eyes, but instead of the usual magic-born-pale-blue, hers were almost purple.

She was all perfect, porcelain, and doll-like. She looked like a little fairy or angel that would sit atop the Christmas tree. Shifter females in general did not possess the ethereal sort of look, we were strong and robust, able to kick butt with a single bound. There was nothing robust about this fae, and yet I sensed an inner strength that would probably match any shifter's.

Nikoli was blinking dazedly at the pretty magic born. He dipped his head. "I'm Nikoli."

She smiled sweetly, full rosy lips and dimples on display. "Rowan."

I didn't want to be rude, but there was no way I was going to let this soup go cold. Not while I was still freezing and starving from our travels here. Finn was already halfway through his bowl.

I smiled at Dalia. "Thank you for the privacy and the meal." I then held up the spoon that had been resting in my bowl. "Please excuse our rudeness. We are half starved. Is it safe to eat?"

She would know what I meant by this. Finn and Nix were creatures of the Otherworld – as apparently were shifters to some degree – but I'd still remain cautious about what we ate here.

Rowan and Dalia nodded, and that's all it took for all of us to dig into our bowls. *Oh. My. gods.* The salty broth slid down my throat and I stopped just short of actually moaning. Kade was inhaling his beside me. After a few huge spoonfuls, I slowed down and took my time, chewing the meat and juicy vegetables, savoring the delicious offering.

Bread arrived to the table, and before I could control my wolf, she'd taken over, snatching up one of the rolls. Pushing her back down with the promise of more food soon, I dipped the bread into the stew and let it soak up the remaining broth. Sir Baladar had probably saved our lives with this aid. I was definitely getting him out of his prison now. Somehow I would find a way.

The food warmed and filled my stomach; contentment like I hadn't felt in days flooded through my body. I would have loved to curl up and go to sleep, but there were some questions I needed answered first. Turning to Dalia – she was eating, but with far less ferocity than the rest of us – I said, "Baladar sent you?"

She nodded. "He spoke with Prince Caspien, told him that the only way to fix the mecca was to get your friend back."

Smart of Baladar, and pretty much true. We did need Violet to fix the mecca, and it would help to motivate the Summer Court in helping us.

"Yes, we believe she's being held by the Winter Court."

Dalia nodded, looking less concerned than I had expected. "We can get you inside the Winter Court. Rowan here has been infiltrating their securities for many years. The prince wanted to come himself, but the king decided that with the current perilous nature of the peace talks between our courts, it was better to stage this to look like a rogue attack and not an orchestrated thing. A resurgence of the war with the Winter Court at this time would ruin our people."

I nodded. "I understand. I'm glad to hear there is less fighting and more peace talks going on for you all." The last time the prince was on Earth, he had spoken of the bitter war between the summer and winter courts. Something had changed in that short time.

I was so grateful to him for his help. We had learned much from the gnomes, but they did not know a lot of the inner workings of the courts. So having a chance to talk to Dalia and Rowan, who could hopefully advise us further about the terrain, dangers, races, and the safety of food, was a huge advantage. I was feeling slightly more confident in our plan already. Plus, with another magic born, we had hugely increased our odds of getting Violet back safely.

For the rest of our time at the table we made small talk, aware of the many fae around us. Winter Court spies would be everywhere. At some point a second bowl of stew was brought to our table. I picked out the chunks of meat and fed Finn under the table. My familiar required a lot more food than me, and needed the extra protein. When the darkness crossed the land, and the hour grew late, we gathered our things to leave.

Dalia waited near a wooden staircase. "We have rooms for all of you. I'll be staying with Rowan in a room just down the hall." *Our own rooms.* And hopefully a shower. I knew from the gnomes village this was a technology not widely available in the Otherworld, but there was something similar they used called a waterfall bath. I had my fingers crossed there was one in this inn.

All of us trudged up to the second floor. Dalia pointed out our rooms. "We will meet you here just after sunrise," the summer fae said. Rowan nodded, standing cloaked at her side. "After a morning meal, we'll set out. There's no time to waste. The Winter Court are not known for their leniency to prisoners."

I swallowed the lump in my throat. I couldn't let myself think about what Violet might be going through. I would actually lose my mind. I kept my focus on rescuing her. Nothing more important than that.

The summer fae disappeared into their room, and I turned to my friends.

"Sleep well," I said, giving each of them a smile, before I entered the second door along the hall. Kade was right behind me.

Blaine and Nikoli were sharing the room on our right, Monica and Victor the one on our left. It was safer to sleep in teams. That way we would not be taken unaware, and all of us being on the same floor was the best for security reasons.

You okay, buddy?

Finn was staying in the stables with Nix. They were acting as our night patrol and first line of defense. We were in Winter Court territory, so there was no way we could completely relax our guards.

All quiet out here. Get some rest, Ari.

Once we were inside the room, doors closed, we set down our packs and weapons near the entrance in case we needed to make a quick escape. Kade went over to tend to the fireplace, stoking the coals until the warmth filled the room. There was another door off to the side, so I strode over and opened it. "Yes!" I let out a low yell, and there might have even been a fist pump or two.

By the time a smiling Kade appeared in the doorway I already had the water flowing from the magically-enhanced showerhead above the wide claw-foot tub.

The bear king lazily assessed me. "You never complain, but I'm guessing her majesty has never had to rough it like this before."

I didn't answer straight away, I was too busy peeling off my furs. When they fell to the floor, followed by my shirt and pants, I glanced up long enough to see Kade's eyes had flashed to molten copper, like perfectly polished pennies.

Straightening, I took one step toward him, wearing nothing but my simple black bra and underwear. "You're right, besides a couple of training exercises, which only last a few hours,

I've always been surrounded by luxury. What about you?"

As his gaze caressed my body, my stomach clenched with need. Without breaking our stare, he shrugged out of his furs, and I paused to enjoy his huge body being slowly revealed, piece by piece, as his clothing fell.

When he spoke, it took every ounce of my concentration to listen. "When my brother went missing, I went rogue. Took off into the world with nothing more than the clothes I wore and two knives. Had to sleep in the forest and hunt for food. I searched for him for a long time, but eventually there was nowhere else I knew to look, so I returned home."

I took another step toward him, wanting to wrap my arms around him. I forgot at times about the brother he lost, the one who was supposed to be king. Kade had no other siblings, and I knew that if I lost Winnie I would never be the same.

Kade was bare-chested now, and the sight of all those chiseled lines had my next question coming out very breathy. "Did you ever find out what happened to him? I mean ... no note? No body? Would he have just left like that?"

Kade closed the distance between us, clad only in cargo pants, top button undone. There was nothing I could have done right then to stop myself from touching him. We had barely had any privacy since being in the Otherworld, and I craved him like nothing I'd ever known before.

His skin was hard and soft at the same time, hot and silky under my touch. A low moan slipped out from between my lips as I slid my fingertips into his pants, and then slowly worked them down his huge body.

He was completely naked under them, and when he answered my question it took me forever to remember I'd even asked one. "He wanted the crown. Kian was always the first in line for anything to do with ruling the bears. He loved his royal life. I can't ever believe he would just up and leave without telling us. I blamed the wolves for a long time, but I always knew deep down it wasn't anything to do with your people."

He slipped my bra off my shoulders before expertly unhooking the clasp. My underwear bottoms disappeared just as fast, and I no longer had any idea what we were talking about.

My body throbbed with need as Kade scooped me up and lowered us into the almost-full bathtub. It was huge, lined with dark tiles that curved near the bottom of the tub. There was a small ledge near the back, and resting upon it was a chunk of freshly cut soap, a few cloths, and what looked like a pumice stone. Grabbing up the soap, Kade dipped it into the water and then started gently rubbing it over my chest, arms, legs.

He rested against the back wall, and I lay across his body as he caressed me. Whomever made this bath so huge deserved a hundred gold coins. Or more. The hot water was like heaven, and I sighed as the scent of something floral and a bit medicinal hit my nose. The soap had some sort of oil in it, made from plants for sure.

After a few minutes, the sight of his huge bronzed hands running across my body was too much for me. I tilted my head back, spinning around to straddle him. Our heavy breathing mingled together, the steam rising around us as our gazes remained locked.

We moved at the same time, our lips clashing with a bruising passion built from days of stress and lack of alone time.

"I love you," I moaned between kisses. He deserved to hear those words every single day, because he was worthy of all the love in the world.

His eyes were beyond dark now, like a whiskey aged to perfection. "You are everything to me, Ari. If anything happens to you, I will destroy this world."

He was serious. I could see that in the darkness of his gaze. "I would do the same for you," I said, pressing my lips to his again.

This kiss sealed our vow that we would follow through, should either of us not make it out of here alive. My worries were buried then as Kade's hand slid along my body and into the water. Worries would not ruin this moment for us, this was about our love, and for now I would take every second I had with my mate. He was my happy place. My everything.

Chapter Five

Winter woes.

THAT NIGHT I slept soundly and reasonably content, considering the circumstances. When I was curled in the arms of my mate, a lot of my worries disappeared. A lot, but not all.

As the early morning hours neared I became restless, tossing and turning, waking and falling back into fitful sleep. The first slivers of light were creeping through the double bay windows of our room when I was sucked into an unnatural, deep slumber. I recognized the sensation straight away; it was another one of those weird dreams. I didn't fight it this time, knowing Violet might be trying to contact me again. A forest sprang up around me, dark and twisty, ancient looking, with a distinctly ominous feel to the air. Turning in a circle, trying to take everything in, I let a gasp escape when a pale figure came into view. Violet. She was quite a distance from me, tied to a tree. The ropes were tight, cutting into her arms, her head hanging limp to one side.

A genuine fear saturated my body as I ran toward my best friend, heart pounding in my chest, her name ripping from my throat in a scream that would haunt me. I could sense no heartbeat, feel no warmth. I thought she was dead until an almost inaudible moan came from her. With what looked like more effort than she was capable of giving, she lifted her head. Her body was bruised and bloody, and there were weird streaks of black ash on her porcelain cheeks.

"Ari..." she whispered as I neared. "Don't touch me,"

Screw that. I knew it was just a dream, but I was going to cut her down. Bending low to the forest floor, I scrambled around until I finally found a rock with a bit of a sharp edge. I then stood ready to saw the bindings that were cutting off the circulation to her arms.

"Don't. Touch. Me," she urgently pressed. "If you touch me, they will know. They will see."

Tears trickled down my cheeks as a sob escaped, followed by a few more. "How can I help? What are they doing to you?"

I couldn't leave her like this. There had to be something I could do.

She took a few deep breaths. Speaking through her pain was clearly hard for her. "Ari, don't trust Isalinda, or Luca, the winter prince. He has a secret ... a dark secret. I got it out of him, by magic and ... I think they're going to kill me."

"No!" My wolf and I both roared, and for a moment I lost control of the beast inside. My hands half shifted, along with my face. I could feel the slight muzzle and sharper teeth. I had to breathe deeply, using every meditation skill I possessed, to get myself back under control. As my bones shifted again, back to normal, I took a step closer to Violet.

"Look at me, Violet." I injected all of my alpha power into that command. "You hold on. Do not give up. You do whatever those royal bastards want you to do. You must stay alive. There are no other options." Her pale eyes never left me, and despite the pure aura of broken she was emitting, I sensed the slightest hope there also. "I'm coming for you, my friend. I'll run the entire way if I have to, without stopping, but I need to know you're still fighting too. I'm not leaving this world without you. Do you understand me? Nothing is more important to me than you."

Violet's eyes were still boring into me, and mingled with the pain and hope were some pure beams of love. She finally gave me a slight nod, wincing as she did. She swallowed roughly before whispering, "The prince—"

"Give him whatever he wants." I was getting desperate now; her protective instincts were going to get her killed.

"He's your father..." Her head went slack as she lost consciousness.

Nothing could have prepared me for what Violet had just said. My entire body had a visceral reaction. My skin tightened, my muscles twitched, and the sound of breaking bones shocked me out of my stupor. The dream was collapsing around me now that Violet was unconscious, and my wolf was reacting to my emotions. Fur sprung up across my arms, bones cracked as my wolf broke free from the cage I'd been keeping her locked down in.

I never planned on shifting in the Otherworld. I had no idea if they could sense the shifter magic here. Too late to worry about it now, there was no controlling either of us in this moment.

Dear God ... my mother had slept with the prince of the Winter Court. I couldn't comprehend how that was even possible, and yet

... Violet would never say something like that unless she was a hundred percent certain. The trees in the dream forest were uprooting now, crashing down around my wolf. She dodged them with her nimble grace, tipping her head back and howling to the darkening sky above. The tree Violet had been tied to remained, but all that was left of my friend was a pile of ropes upon the leaves.

Where had she gone? She couldn't be dead! My wolf howled again. This time it was long and full of mourning.

"Arianna!" Kade's voice broke through the dream and I felt my consciousness rising to wake up.

I was jerked awake, opening my eyes to see Kade with his arms around the sides of my face. Something felt different and it took me a second to realize I had shifted into my wolf in my sleep.

"What's wrong?" His features were broadening and I could see that he too was on the verge of shifting.

I had never been so out of control to let my wolf shift in my sleep. Never! I focused my inner energy toward my beast and she let me have control back. The shift to my human form was fast, giving me just enough time to wonder how I was going to tell the man I loved that I was the offspring of the very people keeping my best friend hostage. A princess of the most warmongering and power hungry court in the fae realm.

Once I was human, naked and lying beside him, I couldn't postpone the truth any longer. Gathering up the sheet, pulling it over myself because I needed the comfort, I sat up and met my mate's eyes.

"It was another dream," I said slowly, my voice trembling. "Violet is ... it's bad. We need to get to her now. Without delay."

He nodded, rubbing a thumb over my hand. "Okay. We'll set out immediately. Is that all?"

He knew. Of course he could feel it. That wasn't all.

I bit my lip and tears fell down my cheeks. Hot, salty, and bitter were my tears, and my heart felt like it was barely even a functioning organ anymore, sluggishly pounding in my chest. I slowly shook my head.

"You can tell me anything," Kade said as he cupped the side of my face and forced me to meet his eyes. "Anything."

I took a steadying breath. "Violet told me that the winter prince, Luca ... is ... my father."

Kade's face did not change, not a single reaction across it, but his eyes were dark and swirly, and his body was as hard as rock. He was upset, and probably shocked. It was not something either of us were prepared for.

Keeping that same calm expression, he leaned forward, pressing his lips gently to mine. "I don't care who your father is, Ari. Or your mother. They aren't you and nothing you could tell me would change the way I feel about you. Or how your people feel about you. All I care about is you … I'm worried about you. Are you okay?"

His instant support and love was more than I'd ever expected. More than I had ever had from anyone, except Winnie, and she loved with the ferocity of a child.

"I'm not sure how I feel," I finally said. "I have no idea how it could have happened. My mind is denying the possibility, and yet it makes sense." I let out a growl. "The shifters will never accept me back as their queen now."

Kade gathered me closer, wrapping his heat and strength around me, lending me his optimism. "Our world is slowly changing. We need to make them see that your father does not matter. It is not who you are."

I didn't say anything more, but both of us knew it wouldn't be as easy as that. Family lines were important in the shifter world, and mine was tainted with darkness. I was part of the enemy.

With a deep breath, I dropped the sheet and forced myself to let go of those immediate worries and focus on Violet. She was my priority. I pressed my face into Kade's hand for a brief second before hopping out of bed. I faced him, naked and vulnerable, but trusting in our bond.

"I love you, more than you could possibly know, and I appreciate your reassurances. Right now, though, we need to regroup and get my best friend back. She's close to death. They are torturing her pretty badly."

He nodded and leapt out of bed to dress. Both of us threw on the first clothes we could find, while I chastised myself for stopping here last night. I loved having some alone time with Kade, but while we were making love Violet was being tortured. It was selfish of me and I just hoped Violet wouldn't pay for my actions. I would not lose focus again, I would not let her down.

"From what you've told me about your mother..." Kade said, breaking me out of my morbid thoughts. "I just can't ever see her having a secret affair with a fae. I would have said it was impossible."

I found him fully dressed, eyes locked on me. He was right, my mother had been a diehard wolf shifter who swore by breeding for society and class. She would never sleep with a fae. There was really only one conclusion I could draw from that.

She wasn't my mother.

Thirty minutes later, after grabbing a quick breakfast and restocking our supplies for the rest of the journey, we left the little village. I told everyone the CliffsNotes version of the dream, leaving out my newly discovered father, and everyone agreed to make the remaining sixteen hour trek without stopping. Dalia and Rowan said it was actually the best way to proceed, because from here on there was pretty much nowhere safe for us. We were right in royal territory now. The winter queen controlled these lands with brutal force.

The plan was that once we reached the outer areas of the castle, we could take turns resting while the others stood guard. Then, in the early hours of tomorrow morning, we would break into their dungeons, or wherever they kept prisoners, and rescue Violet.

Our initial pace was brisk and grueling. No one complained though. Well, not out loud. After about six hours of marching through cold, windswept plains and frozen forests, my body began to protest the abuse. I hadn't felt sore like this in ages. Muscles ached dully. The cold was so brutal it made everything harder. Our metabolisms were in overdrive and there just weren't enough calories to fuel us.

Despite all that, my story of Violet chained to that tree kept us pressing on. Monica had blisters on her feet and she winced with each step but pushed on. They would heal if we could have stopped, but there was no time for that. Finn nuzzled his huge head into my side, offering some of his mecca and energy. It was like a cool balm on a burn, the sweet flow of mecca. Leaning down, I kissed the top of his head, running my hands through his soft pelt. I was grateful to have him here, even though I feared the danger we were all walking into.

For Violet we must press on, he said. I closed my frozen fingers into his fur, allowing his warmth to ease my chill.

Yes, we will save her, and then I'll figure out what to do about my father.

He said no more, but I felt his concern. I understood it, of course. I would feel the same way if it were Finn with the evil megalomaniac parent. It's really unfair that children don't get to choose their parents, because I sure as hell would have asked for a redraw in the genetics lottery. Even if it meant never being a queen heir.

After hours of grueling hiking, the weak sun descended past the horizon, and the darkness of true night fell. Finally Rowan held up a hand to halt us. She had been out in front with Nikoli, scouting for danger, and basically leading the way. At this point we were partially hidden behind some huge rocky crevices, and as I peeked around I could see a huge stone fence in the distance. It looked to tower twenty or more feet into the sky.

"That's the royal village of the Winter Court," Dalia whispered to me. "Within those walls, right at the center, is the castle. The city swells out from there, and everyone who lives in here has sworn their allegiance to the winter queen. Once you are inside, there will be no one to help you."

"You're not coming in with us, right?" I was kind of hoping she had changed her mind.

With a brief smile, she shook her head. "I'm very sorry, I would love to aid you in this, but we cannot be caught close to the main village of the Winter Court. Prince Caspien did request, though, that you visit us in the summer territory before you leave. We will be able to aid your friend's recovery much quicker than back on Earth. Fae magic will probably have been used to contain her, and you'll need fae magic to heal that."

My heart sank at the thought of having to trek a sick Violet all the way back to the Summer Court. I was kind of hoping we could grab her and make a portal and get out of here. But Violet's safety and healing was my top priority and I would do whatever it took.

Everyone was pressed tightly together, waiting for the next move.

"Thank you so much for helping us get this far." I reached out and placed a hand on Dalia's shoulder, and lowered my head in a nod.

She surprised me by pulling me into a hug, before stepping back and saying, "We can stay a little longer so that all of you can rest while Rowan and I keep watch. Just before first light there is a change of the guards. This is your best chance to enter undetected. We'll wake you in time and give you all the tools we can to help."

"Thank you," Kade said, from close to my shoulder. "Our family owes you a debt of gratitude."

Both of the fae shook their heads, gorgeous hair floating around them. So not natural, but a cool trick. "No debt, just make sure you right the mecca and restore the health to the Otherworld. We ask for nothing more."

That I was going to be doing no matter what happened, so I could definitely agree to the deal.

We didn't bother to set up camp, Rowan just used mecca to clean and dry a section of floor in a small cave nearby, and we all snuggled down into our furs, backpacks under our heads. I didn't think I would be able to sleep with my millions of worries – and you know, our comfy stone bed – but my eyes closed the moment my head hit my bag. The day's exhaustion had won. Finn's warmth seeped into my right side, Kade's on my left, fatigue pulled me under, and when Rowan shook me awake, I felt like I had barely slept.

My body was stiff as I stumbled to my feet, stretching out my limbs. I looked around to find Monica, Blaine, Nikoli and Victor in the same half-awake state as me, but no Kade ... or Dalia.

"They're outside," Rowan whispered to me, understanding my rapid scanning of the cave. "Scouting for guards. And Dal is showing him the best way to sneak in."

"Thank you," I whispered back, before quickly ducking outside to freshen up, and then back in again to grab my backpack.

Kade and Dalia still weren't back by the time I was strapped in and ready to go, jerky in hand, chewing through the tough but tasty meat. Of course Kade would sacrifice sleep to make sure he got all the information. It was part of what made him an amazing mate and king. He never let anyone else handle the tough stuff.

I also liked to handle my own battles, and I was annoyed and worried about them being out in enemy land without backup. I had no way to know if they were in trouble or not yet.

Just as my patience ran out and I was about to set out and search, a scuffing indicated someone was approaching. All of us scrambled under bushes and behind boulders. There was no guarantee these were our friends, and it was better to take them by surprise. Sword down at my side, Finn at my back, I would not hesitate to strike if winter soldiers rounded that corner. My people's lives were at stake.

A huge figure stepped in between two frozen trees, icy branches hanging low to form a curtain of sorts. The breath I hadn't even realized I'd been holding whooshed out of me, and I straightened. Kade's eyes dropped to the sword resting against my leg and he gave me a wink and that slow sexy smile that did things to me. Hot and swirly things.

It was kind of sexy that he was proud of me almost attacking him. He never tried to change me, make me act less warrior-like and more stereotypical female.

Nix moved on his shoulder as he waved us forward, and the others slipped free from their hiding spots. Dalia and Rowan both had lines of stress crossing their ageless faces, and I knew they were worried for us.

"We'll wait nearby for your return," Dalia said. "When you make it out, just head toward this cave and we'll find you. Rowan is already working on a distraction so we can all leave the winter territory without issue." Her voice got low and forceful as she drove her final point home. "Remember, this distraction will only work once you are outside the gates. You have to make it out of the village. May the mecca be with you through this journey."

The formality of her final words jolted me into action, and I gave her a nod before sheathing my sword and stepping to Kade's side.

"Let's do this," Monica said, joining me, the others behind her. "We should have enough time to slip in and out before the sun is fully up."

I nodded. The light was still dim, not quite the black of night but not morning yet.

"The guards will change in about ten minutes," Dalia added. "I showed King Kade the way but you need to hurry."

There was no more hesitation. We gave the Summer Court fae one last wave and then Kade was moving. I hurried to keep pace with his long legs. Blaine was on my right and he reached out to briefly squeezed my hand.

"She's going to be okay. Violet is tough. Winter won't break her."

That hot burning in my chest, throat, and eyes was back, but I managed to swallow it down, returning his hand squeeze. Blaine knew better than anyone how much Violet meant to me, how devastated I was inside when I thought about not reaching her in time. It was destroying me, and my stellar ability to compartmentalize things was starting to fail. It almost felt like being this close to her, I could actually feel her pain, and I was desperate to save her.

Kade took us in a loop away from what looked like the main gated entrance and to the eastern side of the wall. As we got closer to the stone barrier, everything was easier to see. Huge pyres were lit along the wall, throwing light across the landscape. Oh, and to highlight the fact that the wall looked utterly impenetrable, huge stone blocks, stacked on top of each other and towering into the air, were staggered with watch towers all around us. I counted at least three fae in each. Kade was keeping us under cover for the time being, sticking to the forest pockets, but we were still about forty yards from the wall, and there was no cover at all in that area. To get closer to the city, we would have to run across the open space and risk being spotted.

How the hell were we going to do that? A guard change could not take any longer than thirty seconds to a minute. If it was anything like ours back in the city, there would be a simple change of position and a brief update of last shift.

Instead of moving us closer, Kade veered off to the right, away from the fenced area. I lost sight of the stone structure as the forest closed in around us, cold air biting into any exposed skin. No one spoke for risk of being discovered, and I was seriously starting to worry about where he was leading us. We seemed to be getting further and further from the main fence. Further from Violet.

We couldn't speak out loud. I could have used the bond, but it would have been distracting and we were in dangerous lands. I halted as Kade's hand shot up into the air. The others stopped also, none of us moving as the bear shifter started creeping along again, making almost no sound. He waved us on then, and we all followed in his exact steps, using the moss and packed dirt to avoid any noisy branches or rocks.

When we were finally behind a large cluster of trees, Kade lifted his hand again and this time pointed to a small gap between two trees. I peered over his shoulder to see that beyond those thick trees was a bare bit of land. A single guard was sitting near a tiny, barred entrance.

Slave entrance, Finn told me. He must have gotten that from Nix. The thought of slaves infuriated me but I let it go, focusing on saving my best friend.

The guard was a tall and menacing looking man, as big as Kade, with two swords crossed over his lap. With his bushy, reddish beard, and heavily muscled arms, he looked like a Viking who could squash a man's head with one hand. Before anyone could ask what the plan was, Kade bent and picked up a small rock. Nix was still on his shoulder and he placed the rock in her beak. Clutching it tightly, she took off, and with barely more than a whisper of wings she flew directly overhead, and I was glad to see that her wing seemed fully healed. Once she was on the opposite side of us, near the far thick wall of forest, she dropped the rock. It made a distinct, loud thump, and the guard was immediately alert, on his feet, both weapons in his hands. He surveyed the land, and we all ducked even lower as he scoped it out.

"Who wants to die today?" the guard called out as he moved further into the packed trees, away from us and toward the area Nix had dropped the stone. Nix kicked it up a notch then, rustling some branches, and the guard started running.

"Let's go," Kade whispered, and then we were sprinting out into the open field. Kade was the first to reach the gated entrance. He swung his head around, features already taking on some of his bear.

"There's a lock!" he growled low.

Before I could even think of what to do next, I was gently pushed aside by Nikoli. The magic born held both hands on the lock and started whispering. A faint purple glow shot out of his hands and the lock clicked. Nikoli took a step back then to let Kade go through first, and I caught sight of his face. He looked worried. *Crap!* Something was bothering the magic born, but I didn't have time to ask what it was. I sensed it was something to do with his powers ... maybe they hadn't worked the way he expected. The lock was open though, which was all that really mattered.

Kade had to hunch himself over to fit through the dark tunnel. There was no time to protest about him taking all the risks. Besides, I had to be fair. If he didn't try to change me, I shouldn't do it to him. Kade was a protector, he would always fight to go first. We all rushed in after him, Blaine bringing up the rear. We made it just in time, shutting the grate and relocking it right before the sound of the guard's approach could be heard.

Nix was going to have to wait for us outside or fly over the top out in the open. I wasn't too worried though, she really couldn't have gone any further with us; she would stand out in the village. Kade could call for her if we needed help.

Cautiously, we crept forward in the darkness. I had one hand resting against Kade's back, and I could feel someone holding my pack. We would not lose each other now, not when we were almost inside. Hopefully. The tunnel was narrow, each side of the walls brushing Kade's shoulders, and he was crouched almost in half to fit.

Up ahead, a flickering of light came into view, and we were even more cautious until we realized it was some lit torches, sitting high in sconces on the wall. They burned with never-dying fire magic, and as we moved past I could see more in the distance. We had enough light now to see attackers if they came at us. Of course, fighting in a confined space like this was another story. Hopefully it wouldn't be a problem.

Finn remained close to my legs. I was having difficulty not tripping over him, but I knew he was staying close for a reason. He was worried, and that worried me. Once we had walked a good distance into the tunnel, Kade stopped and turned around.

"Dalia believes we should be fine now until we reach the city. The tunnels are always empty except for once a month when they bring in new slaves. They just keep the one guard out there as precaution.

"What's the plan?" I asked. My wolf was a bit upset about being underground like this. She was okay when we were walking, but now that we had stopped she wanted to break free. Finn pressed harder against my leg and a small sliver of calmness threaded through me, enough so I could easily push my wolf down again.

Kade got right to it. "We go out in three groups. Arianna is with me. Blaine and Monica. Then Victor and Nikoli, who will travel with Finn."

I didn't like that Finn and I were separated, but I knew there would be a reason, so I waited for the rest. Nikoli took center stage then, the torches lighting up his face in a dance of macabre shadows. "Once I'm inside," he said, "I'll be able to send out a spell that searches for other magic born. This will hopefully lead me to Violet, and also let me know if any other magic users stand in our way. Once I get Violet's general location, I can relay it to Finn and he can pass it on to Ari and King Kade. You guys will be the extraction crew while Victor, Finn, and I take care of any nearby threats."

Blaine shifted forward a little. "What should Monica and I be doing?"

Kade spoke up again, and I was so grateful and relieved that he seemed to have planned this entire thing out. I was far too emotional to do any of it myself, I just wanted to bust in guns blazing and get Violet out.

"The plan is to use this slave tunnel to escape, but I have a feeling that once they know there are intruders and a breakout, they will guard the entrance. So I need you two to find us a backup escape plan. Steal a carriage, some horses, dig a tunnel, make a distraction … whatever you have to do."

Monica had a fierce look in her eye. Her strategic mind was already at work, trying to figure out how to get us out of here. "You got it, Your Majesty. We will not let you down."

I was so proud of my friends, my pack. "Stay safe, everyone. Let's bring Violet home," I said, holding my hand out. One by one, they laid their hands on top of mine, like a football team right before heading out onto the field. If only this were a game and not a fight for our lives.

Our tender moment broke up too quickly, then Nikoli was stepping forward and taking the lead. It was time to get my best friend back.

The slave tunnel exited into a stone alleyway. Kade and I were waiting at the entrance, giving Nikoli and his group time to make it out into the open court of the winter palace. The magic born was using a basic disguise again. Conserving all of his energy was important. He had admitted just before disappearing that he felt weak, that opening that lock had taxed him, which was what I had suspected from his concerned look earlier. It was odd though. I was feeling stronger than ever.

The mecca feels more intense here, I said to Kade as we waited.

He wrapped his arm around my shoulders, pulling me into him. I rested against him briefly and felt his lips brush my hair. *Yes, they must build their royal villages over the stones. Like we do with our boroughs.*

That made sense. Even with the energy low in the Otherworld, there was still a decent source somewhere here. I could feel it thrumming through my body, energizing me in a way I hadn't felt since coming here.

Let's go, Kade said, and I pulled away from him, brushing down my furred cloak. We would have to blend in and act calm until we received word from Nikoli. It was time to get Violet back.

Chapter Six

Familiar faces in the crowd.

ACTING CASUAL, WE both strolled from the alley and found ourselves skirting the outer areas of a marketplace. We moved straight into the fray; the best way to blend in was to be in plain sight and act like a local. Thankfully a lot of the highborn fae I could see were tall, and plenty wore thick cloaks and furs with hoods to guard against the cold, so Kade and I did not stand out. We strolled casually into the crowds, stopping periodically to examine some of the crafts and wares on display. We could do nothing else until we received word from Finn.

"This is beautiful," I said to a merchant, running my hand over a clay comb and mirror set.

The woman bowed slightly and muttered her thanks to me. Kade and I moved on to another stall, and I was getting anxious for word of where Violet was. Had Nikoli been caught? Was he having trouble with the spell? Even if they had been caught, Finn should be able to let me know ... unless strong magic was involved.

Just when I was about to lose my mind, I felt my familiar's energy. *Okay, he's got her location pinpointed.*

Thank the shifter gods!

Show me, I said. I knew he would understand my meaning. Instead of using words, he opened his mind wider to me. This way I would get images, and his thoughts that went with each one.

A huge stone structure came into view and I knew without him saying that this was the castle. It looked like a dark version of a stereotypical fairytale palace: moats, turrets, dark stone, and wandering ivy all along the sides.

Finn didn't linger on any one image for too long. He rushed past the entrance and showed me that just inside the inner palace gates, over the moat that surrounded the entire building, there were two paths. The one to the left was the worker and slave entrance. If we took that, it would lead us right inside, like a ramp that traversed the many floors of the castle. Violet was being kept on the lowest level in the dungeon.

Finn let me know that Nikoli didn't think she was heavily guarded, because she was gravely injured; her light was dim. They wouldn't bother with many guards. I took a steadying breath, relaying everything to Kade through our bond. He nodded, and without another word we took off briskly through the village toward the open gates of the main palace.

I was barely paying attention to my surroundings, focused on the path I needed to take to Violet. As we turned a corner, about to cross over the raised bridge across the moat, my eyes alighted on a familiar looking fae.

It was just a brief second of eye contact with a mountain of a man who had been bent down on one knee helping a young boy with his shoe. He had been staring at me as hard as I was staring at him, as if also trying to place me … or was he staring at Kade?

Before I could say anything, maybe ask Kade if he recognized him, we were already out of sight, moving over the iced dirty water and through the gates of the royal estate. The fork in the path was right at the entrance, and we took the left as instructed. Walking along the cobblestones, I noticed a man wheeling a cartful of scones, biscuits, and even what looked like bagels.

"Kade," I whispered, giving a quick head nod toward the pastry guy.

Kade immediately got my intentions, moving straight across to him. "Sir?"

The man stopped and took in Kade, his eyes lingering on the shiny sword, before he looked fearfully between us both.

"Yes?" he inquired in a shaky voice.

Kade was close enough now to touch him. He reached into his coat and pulled out the coins Dalia had given us. "A bag of coins for your cart. Just leave now, speak of this to no one, and enjoy the gold."

The man's eyes widened, his brow furrowed as he eyed the stack of coins in Kade's outstretched palm. He was a shorter, overweight fae, with tired eyes. I was guessing this was more money than he had seen in a lifetime, but still he took an uncomfortably long amount of time to decide. Kade remained calm, never showing any unease. I wasn't hiding my impatience nearly as well, desperate to get to Violet, but I knew that a disguise would be very helpful, so I kept myself busy by watching our backs. A few people were milling about in the distance, but for now we were alone. Which was good, because if this man said no we would have to knock him out to keep him from talking.

Thankfully, the coins won out; he scooped them up before turning and walking away, leaving his cart of goods without so much as a look over his shoulder. Kade slipped his sword off and I followed suit, stashing them in the bottom of the cart and throwing our coats over them. I pulled my hair from its braid and ratted it up a bit, kneeling down to scoop some of the flour from the cart shelf, wiping it on my nose and on Kade's shirt. Did we look like bakers? Probably not, but it was the best we could do with what we had.

It didn't require two people to push the cart, so I let Kade take it. He was the one who stood out the most with his height and the scary vibe he naturally had. I hurried along close by, head lowered like I was just a slave or helper.

The path was not busy, so we made it inside the palace without an issue. I kept Finn's directions firmly in my head and relayed them to Kade so he'd know which way to go. To get to the dungeon we would have to use the servants' hallway, which was a long, winding, ramp-style descent, wide enough to allow others to pass coming the opposite way, but still wedged into the back of the palace. Everyone we passed looked a little browbeaten; no one was paying much attention to each other, remnants of a hard life creased across all of their faces despite the faes' ability to remain young looking forever.

The cart pushed easily down the ramp. The floor was very hard, like concrete, or compressed dirt. As we neared the lower levels, clanking could be heard. That had to be the dungeons.

This castle was huge. We had probably passed five floors on our descent, before we reached the prison section. It was much colder down here. Without my cloak my hands were shaking, my steps stiff. The clanking grew louder, and for the first time I saw someone other than a plain-dressed server-fae moving along our path. A guard, dressed in heavy white furs, which Finn told me were the royal color and uniform.

Kade lowered his head and I did the same, and the guard continued stomping past, his sword swinging wildly from where it was sheathed in his belt-scabbard. I was just lifting my head up again, relieved to be past him, when the guard called something to us in a language I did not understand. Kade and I paused, keeping up our charade in the hopes we could talk our way out of this. If we were caught out now, they would alert all the guards, and it would be much harder to reach Violet.

Brushing my hair down to make sure my ears were covered, I spun around and bowed my head low. The guard took a step toward me and I could feel Kade tensing at my back. Raising my head, I blinked rapidly and forced my face into a blank stare. Acting stupid got plenty of people out of trouble. Being stupid got them into it, though, so you had to be careful about how much of it was an act.

"I'm sorry, sir." I kept my voice low and trembly. I knew they spoke English here, I had heard it many times. Hopefully he didn't think it was odd for us to use it.

The guard switched to English easily. "I said, What are you doing down here? The baked goods go to floor five, near the kitchens."

His accent was heavy, the words slow. I tried desperately to think of something to say. "We were sent down with treats for the guards."

Everyone loved treats, right? Kade shifted his big body closer. It felt like he was part of the stone wall behind me he was that tense. I could feel very low rumbles rocking his chest.

The guard took another few steps toward me. I could see him much better now, the way his closely-set eyes focused on my body, especially around my chest and thighs. He gave off all the creepy vibes, from his overly shiny bald head to the yellow tinge of those eyes.

"We really need to move, sir." It was really hard for me to keep my voice low and sweet. I pretty much just wanted to knee him in the balls, and he had come close enough for me to reach without a problem.

He leaned over until our faces were inches apart. "The queen would never allow a call for treats. The guards are here to work, not eat. But I'll let it slide if you come with me now, just for a quick chat, without your big friend."

My hand moved before my brain caught up. I pulled my arm back and punched him in the throat, one solid blow that knocked him backwards and left him wheezing on the floor. Before I could finish the job, Kade turned and slammed his fist down into the guard's temple, knocking him out cold. I quickly spun around to make sure no one had seen, and was relieved to see we were alone on the ramp. I tentatively reached out and ran a palm up Kade's arm.

"It's okay. I hit him before he could alert anyone."

My mate's body was trembling, on the verge of losing control of his bear and shifting. In a quick burst, I found myself crushed against his hard body. "He was going to touch you," he growled. "I don't have time right now to kill him and hide the body, which is the only reason he's still alive."

I chuckled. It was strained but it counted. "Well, we do still have to hide the body.

Otherwise someone will alert the other guards much faster.”

He gave me one last squeeze before stepping away. “I saw a small supply room a few floors above us. Wait right here and I’ll be back in a minute.”

I nodded, and he turned to roughly haul the guard up and over his shoulder. With a quick glance around to make sure no one else was coming down the path, he took off at a sprint, long legs eating up the distance, until I could no longer see him on the servers’ path. I hunched forward over the cart, pretending to rearrange the pastries and such. A young girl startled me as she burst from the door across the hall. As she hurried past me I noticed the red welt marks across her green tinged skin. I prepared myself for some questions, but thankfully she didn’t even glance across in my direction.

Come on, Kade.

I was mentally urging him on, which of course I had forgotten he could hear.

On my way, woman. Give a bear a minute to hide a body.

I had to hide my chuckles in my hand, otherwise I’d look like the crazy lady laughing at nothing.

Why do I have the feeling we might be having this exact same conversation multiple times over our life together?

He sent me back a bunch of images of him in the woods, axe in hand, chasing down intruders. Well, at least I think that's who he was chasing, because I lost all train of thought at the sight of my lumberjack mate. Holy sweet nectar of life, Kade was so goddamn hot. Almost unfair, really.

Before I completely lost my mind, he was back, and in a stroke of genius was wearing the guard's uniform, white furs and all.

"Brilliant," I whispered, because we had really been pushing it expecting people to believe an almost seven foot tall, ripped warrior-looking guy was here to give out scones.

We started moving again. We were close to Violet. I could feel her unique magic. A magic which had been part of my life since before I could remember. A magic and person I could not live without. Rounding the final corner of the servants' ramp that led to the dungeons, I saw two large guards at the door. Violet's energy pulsed then, I could feel it. She knew I was near and was reaching out.

"Forgive me," Kade whispered to me, before he abandoned the cart and grabbed me by the hair. I immediately knew where he was going with it, so I cried out. His hold didn't hurt, he was barely pulling, but I had to play my part convincingly.

My scream brought the attention of the guards.

Kade called out down the hallway: "This one was caught stealing from the queen. She's to be locked up until her punishment is decided."

I kept my head low and made a painful face, letting out a distressed whimper.

"Please don't," I begged. "I just wanted some extra food for my family."

One of the guards was walking toward us now. He scanned Kade briefly, before focusing on me. "We're all hungry! That doesn't give you the right to take what the queen has paid for!" He was pretty much shouting in my face, and I could feel Kade tensing even further. I just hoped he could keep his bear under control until we got inside.

The guard, apparently done with his show of dominance, turned to his buddy. "Open it up!" Then he grabbed my arm, trying to take me from Kade.

This time Kade's grip did tighten on my hair, to a painful level. "She's mine. She kicked me in the manhood when I tried to catch her. She's gonna get some payback." He growled at the guard, one of his more menacing rumbles.

The guard paled a little, before recovering some of his previous arrogance. He let out a rattle of a chuckle. "I understand. Take her in."

Kade had to duck his head to step through the low doorway, making sure to keep a tight hold on me in case the guards were watching us. As soon as we were farther inside, the heavy door clanked behind us and I relaxed a little.

Hang on, Vi! We're coming.

Kade let me go when we reached a short set of stairs. There was no other path, so we moved down. From below I could hear moaning and faint screams, and it sent chills up my arms.

"Are you okay?" Kade ran his hands through my hair gently, dropping them to my shoulders for a brief rub.

I nodded, reaching up to give his hand a quick squeeze. "Let's go get her."

He grabbed my arm, underneath the armpit, and proceeded to descend the steps with me. We would keep up this guard and slave charade for as long as it worked. As we dropped off the last step into a dark hallway, I could see a row of large arched stone doorways, each with heavy bars across them.

I wanted to scream Violet's name, but only a few doors down a guard was sitting on a chair reading something. As we neared, he looked up and I immediately focused on the set of keys visible in his pocket. A few silver keys had fallen out, glinting in the fire lights. Kade must have seen it too, because he called the guy over.

"Hey, you won't believe this. Come look." He pointed to something on my neck.

The guard looked intrigued, standing to walk the three short paces to us. The second he was in arm's reach, Kade dropped my arm and slammed the fae's head into the wall. It bounced off with a wet thud and the guard landed heavily on the floor. Kade knelt and scooped up the keys from the guard's pocket.

Kade and I made quick work of getting the guard back in his chair, draping him against the wall so it looked like he was having a quick nap. Then I ran down the hall, whisper-screaming Violet's name, peering in each of the cells, which were full. But none held my friend. Finally, near the end farthest from the stairs we'd used to enter, I heard a faint response.

"Ari!" A weak sob followed my name. Kade had his borrowed sword unsheathed and was running after me, ready to cut down anyone who got in my way.

I passed the last few cells, glancing in to find mostly women and children, but no Violet. Seeing the browbeaten fae had my blood boiling, but I couldn't focus on that. Finally, white hair came into sight – well, mostly white ... a lot of it was streaked with dirt ... or blood, the old, dried kind that turns a dark brown-maroon. She was strung up by metal chains attached to the stone walls, hanging limply, just like in my dream.

"I'm here, Vi!" I shouted.

Kade quickly fit one of the keys into the lock and it clicked open. With ease he slammed the heavy door open and I burst into the room. Scents assaulted me, human waste and torture, which I fought to ignore.

After a quick survey of the cell, to make sure we were alone – the room was empty except for a small table that held a dome glass artifact similar to a snow globe – I ran to Violet. My hands were shaking as I waited for Kade to uncuff her. Her skin was so ashen it worried me.

"Don't touch me or their magic born will see," she whimpered, eyes still shut.

My teeth gritted, I forced words through my rigid jaw. "Let them see." I wanted to kill everyone responsible for this treatment of Violet. Let them send their magic born so they could meet their death.

I placed one hand on Violet's wrist to steady her arm for unlocking the cuff, and received a little jolt, a shock that ran down my arm and dissipated. Kade growled behind me.

"What was that?" he murmured.

"You felt that?"

He tried the first key but it didn't work, before he moved on to the next, trying them all one by one.

"Yes, it felt like mecca."

My words were hurried: "It was probably the spell the magic born put on her. Now they know we're here."

Get ready for the exit plan. I've got Violet, I said to Finn.

Finn's reply came back rapidly. *I know. Nikoli is fighting one of the magic born right now.*

Crap. We needed to go. Finally the fourth key worked. As Kade undid the cuffs, Violet fell into my arms like a sack of flour. My mate gave me a look that said we needed to hurry, and he went back to stand guard at the door.

"You came for me." Violet's voice was weak, and I could sense she was completely drained of power. Whatever they had done to her was beyond physical torture; they had also drained her of magic and essence. Those bastards.

"Always," I told her, hugging her so tightly I was sure I would break her. Kade spun back then and scooped Violet into his arms, throwing her gently over his left shoulder, which allowed him to keep his right hand free to fight with his sword.

"Guards are moving, we need to go," he said. Violet squirmed on Kade's shoulder, protesting.

"No, Ari. The glass ... you have to touch it. You have to take your essence back or they will do bad things with it." Her tone was as forced as she could manage in her weakened state, but I knew it was important to her. This was the glass she'd spoken about in the dream, that she said contained my energy...

I walked toward it hesitantly, examining it more closely. I hadn't paid attention before, but as I stood before it, the true beauty within astonished me. The glass itself was probably only ten inches tall and half that size wide. It had a detailed silver base that wrapped up around the bottom of the domed glass. From a distance, when I'd first glanced at it, I thought it was empty. But it wasn't.

A turquoise mist was swirling in slow arcs around the center of the glass, tinged through with a silver and gold that reminded me of the color of my eyes. As I stepped even closer, no more than an inch from the glass, my hand began to shake, the hairs on my arms stood up, and I felt this aching in my heart. It was not an ache I had ever felt before. It was almost like a huge cavern existed inside of me, and somehow I had never noticed it.

I was not whole.

I needed to be whole.

Until this very moment I had not known I was half-empty, but there was no way to shut that ache down. I inhaled deeply, and was shocked to find that it smelled of me, felt like me. The silver mists shifted, and I blinked a few times as I wondered if what I was seeing was real. There was an image, familiar to me, the day Finn had arrived in my life when I was five. The massive familiar bonded to a tiny, white-haired wolf-shifter. Another swirl and a new image appeared: my first time on the Island with Blaine and Violet. The next was the day my sister was born and my mother was no longer with me. Over and over, images of my life flashed in the dome, and there was no doubt this energy was tied to me. To my life.

Violet was right. Whatever this glowing turquoise energy was … it was mine.

Unable to stop myself, and knowing time was running out, I wrapped both hands around the glass, intending to pull it up and release the contents. However, the moment I touched it, a shockwave ripped through me and the glass began vibrating in my hands. I couldn't let it go now even if I wanted to. My body was shaking as hard as the glass.

A cracking sound filled the cell and the turquoise energy pulsed out, growing larger as the glass shattered. With force strong enough to shoot me backwards across the room, the dome exploded, glass spraying everywhere. The turquoise energy slammed into my body, filling up all the parts of me that were empty.

The breath knocked out of me, I struggled to sit up. I expected to be cut to shreds, but there wasn't one mark on me from the explosion of glass.

I sat there getting my bearings for a moment. My breath was back now, but my insides were swirling strangely. The vibration had not stopped, it had only moved internally. A burst of heat and life shot through my center, through the part of me that had been aching and empty only moments before. I cried out as my head dropped back against the wall, my hands scraping over the dirty stone floor.

"Ari? Talk to me!" Kade rumbled.

The urgency in his voice snapped me out of whatever weirdness was holding me in its grasp. I was able to focus again – well, sort of. I felt like myself, but also ... different. I felt alive.

Adrenaline coursing through me, I jumped to my feet. Shifter energy, mecca, and something else mingled within my center. Some new great power was coursing through my body. I hurried across to Kade. He was staring out into the hall, preparing for an impending attack. Dropping my hand onto his biceps, I said, "I'm okay. Let's get out of here."

He swung his head around to see me, and even though he tried to hide it, his eyes widened and his jaw went a little slack. Shock. Not something he normally displayed.

I looked behind me, wondering what he was seeing.

"Ari … your ears," he finally said. His tone was one part shock and two parts awe.

I inhaled quickly as my fingers came up to feel my ears. Oh … my … the tips were pointed like a full highborn fae.

"I'm a fae," I said to the room, needing to say it out loud so I could try and wrap my head around it.

A clanking of metal had us all focusing; Kade was again in warrior mode. "Stay close behind me, Ari. We need to move fast."

I swallowed hard, trying my best to ignore that I now had pointy ears, and some new fae magic was swirling inside me, its heat filling me with a life and vibrancy I had never felt before.

Holy crap … I was fae.

Chapter Seven

The wheels of time are often jagged.

KADE WAS ALREADY moving and I stayed right on his heels. Violet must have passed out, because she was limp over his shoulder, but her breathing sounded calm and rhythmic, which was a small relief. The path through the cells was clear, but that part was always going to be easy. It was the part where we had to get past the guards, through the castle, out of royal territory, and then out of the Winter Court, which was going to be a problem.

A problem which was starting in three ... two ... one. *Showtime.*

Two guards popped into view, one on either side of the stone entranceway. They held huge swords, but with the narrow confines of the corridor, it was going to be hard for them to use that style of weapon effectively. Without missing a beat, Kade slid Violet to me. I took her weight with ease, and then he attacked, rushing straight in, his own sword out in front.

Now, I had seen Kade fight a few times, and most of those times had been against fae, but I had never seen him fight this close up. Usually I was fighting as well, so my attention was divided. Not now though. Now I got to watch it without distraction.

He was a thing of beauty. Kade was a huge guy but you'd never know it with the way he ducked the first attack from Guard One, then straightened to deliver a knockout blow to Guard Two, who definitely had not been prepared for his speed, grace, and brawn rolled into one package. Guard One then spun, also reacting far too slowly, and ended up with an elbow in his throat. He dropped, grasping at his neck, struggling to breathe, and Kade finished him off with a kick to the temple.

Holding Violet as gently as I could, her weight was not a problem for me. It was more about maneuvering her length without smashing her head into things. I leapt over the fallen guards and we were up the stairs and out of the cells, back out on the ramped path. As we dashed toward the cart, which was still sitting there,

Kade lifted Violet from me, allowing me time to grab the furs and our elven swords that had been resting underneath.

We didn't stop moving. Besides a few servants who didn't look our way, the path remained surprisingly unoccupied. We'd definitely chosen the right way to enter the castle. This ramp did not seem to be used by any highborn fae. I was pretty sure it had been unlucky that we'd run into that one guard on the way down – unlucky for him that was.

As we were emerging out of the castle, into the icy outside, Kade blocked my view for a second. I tried to see our surroundings as best as I could. Kind of looked like everything was free from guards here too.

Ambush? I asked him mentally, before sending a quick message to Finn. *We're out. Looks clear so far. Should we be expecting anything?*

Kade answered me first, out loud. "I can't sense anything, Ari, but that in itself makes me suspicious. We know they felt Violet when you touched her, so they know we're here. So why have they let us get this far?"

Unfortunately that was not a question I had an answer to. "Well, we have no choice but to head for the others. Hopefully luck is on our side today."

We started moving. Finn's reply of *We're waiting here,* had an image attached to it. They were at a small hut just off to the side of the main gate. *Merchant cart. Lots of silk and material to hide beneath.*

Why is no one chasing us? Where are the magic born? I asked him.

Nikoli took one down, and I disabled the other. So far no more have shown themselves. Hurry, Ari, we have a clear run right now, but the gates will be more heavily armed once word reaches that their magic born have been disabled.

Be there soon.

I shut him out of my mind so I could focus. Kade and I moved side by side. Violet was still over his shoulder, I had draped his extra furs over her for both warmth and to hide her. Both of us sheathed our swords and then hurried out into the bustling world of the Winter Court. We made it through those palace gates and over the small bridge without a problem. We slowed through the marketplace, which was thankfully far less busy than earlier. It looked like most of the merchants were packing up, which was probably why Finn thought this was a good time to bail. If we left in the silks cart with all the other merchants, there was less chance of discovery.

I found myself looking at the faces we passed. For some reason, the man I had seen when we were entering, the one tying the little boy's shoe, was still bothering me. I knew him ... or he knew me. There was a spark of recognition there, and now that I was mostly fae, I wondered if he was family ... or something else.

I was fae! I had almost forgotten that. Had more changed than just my ears? Hopefully, If we lived through this, I'd be able to find a mirror and check out my new look. As Kade turned toward the old pipe entrance we had used to get in here, I realized he didn't know the new plan. I grabbed his arm to slow his steps, before sending him mental pictures of our new rendezvous point. He gave me a nod, swiveling and heading in the opposite direction. We walked fast, but not fast enough to draw attention. My eyes were constantly on the move, trying to determine where the guards and possible ambush might come from.

The large, double-gated stone entrance came into view. The path widened, and there were fewer houses scattered around us. The building Finn had shown me also came into view, and I was relieved to duck in and get away from the open, striding under some brightly colored shade awnings and into another alley, this one large and well lit.

The cart was sitting there with two horse-like creatures tethered to the front. The canvas that looped up and over the back of the structure covering it was bright and silky, the color a mix of purples and blues. Blaine popped into view; he'd been crouched down beside one of the horses.

His face lit up when he saw me. He took two huge strides to scoop me up into his arms. "Thank the gods you're safe. And perfect timing. The merchants are leaving for the night."

I hugged him back just as tightly, so relieved that everyone was okay. So far.

By the time I had pulled back, Kade had disappeared, already around the back of the cart to stow Violet inside. My eyes met Blaine's, and I could see his surprise as he looked me over and settled on my ears.

My smile felt wonky. "I'll explain everything later. For now we need to get going."

Monica was close by, and even though her eyes were wide too as they ran across me, she didn't say anything. I wasn't the only one with a new look. She was dressed like a mystic, bracelets up her arms, beads and a yellow silk scarf woven into her hair.

"Whoa," I said, a more genuine smile ripping across my face. "You look gorgeous."

She gave me a wink. "I'm the silk merchant, don't you know? Time now to get us out of here."

"I'll sit with you," I offered. "Since, you know … I'm now very fae-like."

I could see the million questions in her gaze, but she didn't ask. Blaine didn't either, clasping a hand on my shoulder, before taking his place in the back of the cart too.

All good in there? I asked Kade and Finn.

Yep, was the reply from both, and I scrambled up onto the bench seat with Monica. She took the reins in her hands, and now it was time to get these fae-spec horses on the road. We had rescued my friend, and the Summer Court would heal her, but only if we could make it outside of these walls.

Monica clicked her tongue and the horses began to walk. At first it was a very tight fit, trying to maneuver along the path between the houses. Monica was skilled at pulling the reins and aligning the horses on the perfect path. We finally emerged onto the main road, about a hundred yards from the gate.

My palms were clammy as I clutched the small side rail. I don't think I'd ever been this nervous. The clip clopping of the horses' hooves fell into the same rhythm as the hammering of my heart as we closed in on the gate. There looked to be a lot of guards there now, checking out the long line of carts exiting. Had there been that many when we entered? I hadn't paid that much attention.

Monica and I shared a look. This could quite possibly go south, but Violet was near death and I wouldn't let my best friend die.

"Monica, do you still consider me your queen?" I asked her in a low voice.

She paled. "Yes, of course."

I let my wolf peer out of my eyes when I gave the command: "Then it's my order that if things go bad, you ride this cart as hard and fast as you can to get Violet healed. You find Dalia, you get to the Summer Court, and you do not stop for anything or anyone. Including me. Can you do that for me?"

She gritted her teeth, her body shaking, her wolf peering out through her eyes. "But—"

There was no time for her hesitation. "Monica, she's hurt really bad. Like may not make it through the night bad."

Monica nodded, her spine straightening as she took the weight of the burden I had dropped on her. She understood, and I was confident she would follow my orders.

We were close enough to hear the guards now. "Move along!" one of them shouted to a cart in front of us.

I fixed a pleasant expression on my face as they moved on to us. A giant of a fae stepped forward, his heavy furs making him look unnaturally large. His eyes roamed over Monica and I, then he walked to the back of the cart. My body tensed. I was ready. If there was a struggle I would jump off and fight.

Nikoli must have spelled an illusion though, because after a few minutes poking around in there, the guard strode back to my side and nodded. "Move along!"

The way in front of the cart was clear, and Monica kicked the horses into gear. I smiled at the guard, keeping up the illusion, but a sliver of hope was thrumming inside of me. We were almost in the clear. Now we just had to get to Dalia before Violet got any worse. Hopefully Nikoli was doing something back there to help her while we traveled, although I had no doubt he was completely spent from fighting off the other magic born.

Any speck of hope I had dissipated when a shout was let out close by. "It's her!"

The voice had been female, and following it was a blast of magic that hit me in the back of the neck, knocking me from the cart.

I tumbled to the rough ground, my neck burning from whatever had hit me. I was stunned but not incapacitated as I jumped to my feet. "GO!" I shouted to Monica as I unsheathed my sword.

A woman in long, dark furs, her hair midnight black, offsetting bluer-than-blue eyes, lifted both hands and flung magic at the cart to stop it. *Holy crap.* She was magic born, but there was no lack of pigmentation going on with her. She was a wash of both dark and light.

Her first shot missed the cart, and as she geared up for the second one, I was readying a shield.

Finn reacted then. I felt him connect to me and I knew he was about to jump out and help. *Finn! I need you to stay with them, to make sure Violet is okay. Promise me. I'll keep this magic user busy and then find a way to get out.*

He howled in our bond, his pain tangible, but he didn't fight me. He trusted me to look after myself, and that belief in me was like a burst of energy.

I will go with them, Ari, and make sure Violet is safe. But if you're not out after that, I'm coming for you. I will kill them all.

I love you. Stay safe.

I missed his reply as the woman threw a second mecca ball of magic toward the retreating cart, and that's when I dove to intercept it, shield up.

It crashed against my energy shield and dissipated. Hah! If I wasn't fighting for my life, I would have been excited to have finally mastered that technique Kade had taught me.

Crap, Kade! In my rush of adrenalin I had stopped shielding my mind from him, which meant...

Nix's cry rang out from the sky and suddenly a warm familiar presence was at my back. I should have known he would not leave my side, never leave me in the enemy's hands. Guards were closing in on us, and one quick peek over my shoulder told me that Monica was past them and out the gates. They would make the rendezvous point with the summer fae no problem. Violet would get the help she needed.

Turning back to my enemy, the magic born was sizing up Kade and I. In a flash we were surrounded by at least twenty guards, all armed to fight. The dark-haired fae spoke to the closest one. "Inform the queen that we have her. Put the female in the dungeons and sell the male at the market tonight. He will make someone very, very happy. Big and muscled, a perfect workhorse." Her grin was broad and creepy, with teeth that were slightly pointy, like they had been filed.

Don't reveal your power. They will kill you if they think you're a threat, I said to Kade. *Go with them now. We'll figure out how to escape and meet up.*

If this magic born knew he could manipulate mecca, he was done for.

A rumble sounded in his chest. *I'm not leaving your side.*

Kade!

I heard the ripping of muscles and knew he was shifting into his bear form. He was going to try to take them all out. Dammit. Maybe he could. If I could take on the magic born, he could get the guards.

Just as I was feeling hopeful, a chill rose up and a fog rolled in. Riding on a sparkling white horse was the most beautiful and terrifying woman I had ever seen. Long white hair floating behind her like a silk sheet, huge eyes that were so dark they looked black. She was thin but muscled as she gripped her horse, riding bareback, no need for a saddle.

Kade was nearly in his bear form now; his shifts were getting faster every time. One of the guards advanced on him. I stepped forward and sliced the guard's arm, then his chest, and he fell back. Spinning around, I prepared myself to fight the white-haired demon woman. She was almost to us, and a hush fell over the entire area as every single guard went to one knee, including the magic born.

Kade, as a bear, roared so loud it made my eardrums shake. The woman, who I assumed to be the queen, raised her left hand and pointed it at Kade.

"Freeze," she whispered, icy fog misting from her blue-tinged lips. Kade's roar was cut off mid-bellow; he stopped moving as his dark fur was slowly covered in a film of ice.

My next move wasn't my brightest, but I was a hotheaded woman and she'd just frozen my mate. I gave a battle cry and lunged for her and her horse, sword raised, mecca crackling along my skin.

"*Brista,*" the Queen said, and thick blue magical bands wrapped around my arms and legs, shutting my mecca power off like a light switch. I went down, hard, my legs pulled out from under me. My face hit the ground with a solid thud, sending a shooting pain through my skull. The world went a little dark around the edges as I fought to remain conscious.

The queen came closer, her voice still breathy, like it was made from flurries of ice and snow. "A bear shifter ... he will fetch me a fortune at auction. Take him away and then put her in the same cell her friend was in."

As the magic born snapped her fingers, I was lifted magically into the air, and I saw that man again, the one I had sort of recognized earlier. He was in a crowd of fae onlookers, his face etched with lines of worry as he watched Kade and me.

Holy ... what the hell? It hit me hard then, the reason his face had been bothering me. He looked like Kade and Annette, Kade's mother. So either they had some very close fae relatives that none of us knew about or that was his brother. Living in the Winter Court ... with a child.

A guard hoisted me up and my head smashed into his hard shoulder. That blow was enough for me to lose the last of my consciousness, and before I could cry out or fight, the world went dark.

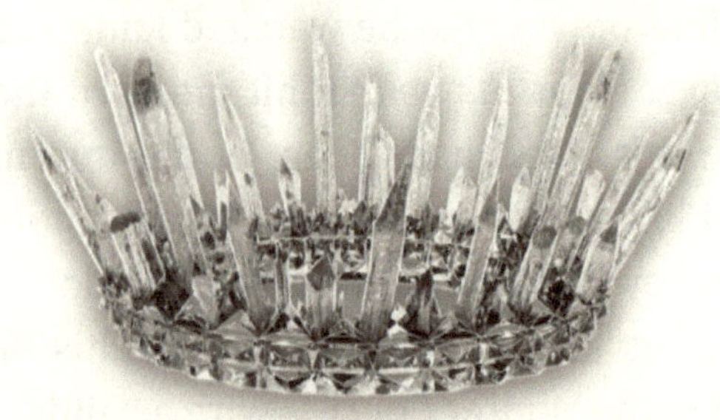

Chapter Eight

Daddy dearest.

CLANKING NOISES ROUSED me, the metallic sharpness reverberating through my aching head. I was face down with a musty bedding of straw beneath me – pretty much the only thing keeping me from lying against icy stone. Remembering that I had been taken by the winter queen, I tried to get my eyes open and head up, but the moment I moved, my stomach lurched and I let myself slump forward again as I fought to control my gag reflex.

My wolf stirred lazily within me, which was my first indication that there was something wrong with her. Normally she would be fighting to change, to heal whatever was ailing me, but it was almost like she was barely conscious. And my mecca was the same.

A strange energy caught my attention. It was the only thing within my center of energy that didn't seem to be under the influence of the queen's magic right now. *I'm fae.* Whatever had been in the glass jar, whatever essence had been stolen from me as a child, was strong. And the winter queen wanted it.

I needed to shift. I tried to coax my wolf forward, but she only whined at me, which hurt my heart in ways I couldn't understand. What had the queen done to us? As if she felt my desperation and sorrow, my wolf spirit started clawing toward me. I could almost see her in my mind's eye. I needed to touch her. The fae energy inside me burst to life then – it was warm and yet somehow icy at the same time – as if it were reacting to my thoughts. Barrels of energy smashed into my beast, freeing her. The shift washed over me and in a flash I was a wolf. No pain. No messy breaking of bones or minutes of panting. Just the simple thought and I could change.

Shaking off the last of my aches and fatigue with ease, I was up on all fours, my white coat reflecting the dim prison lighting. For the first time since waking I was warm all the way through, and my energy was slowly returning.

The pit of fae power deep inside of me flooded across my body. It was like it had been contained until now, but the moment I used it, freed it, an icy fire had spread across my chest and through my limbs, morphing me, changing the essence of who I was.

Winter magic.

Clanking sounded again, and a figure appeared in front of the barred door of my cell. It was the queen, accompanied by two guards, forming a massive wall of muscle on either side of her.

"Nice to see you're awake, Granddaughter."

She sneered on that last word, and it was very clear she did not welcome our familial bonds. *That makes two of us, bitch.* My wolf dropped lower, snarls ripping free, fangs bared. The queen waved her hand at me, then ice seeped through the bars and my body was frozen again. Well, sort of. It wasn't as all-encompassing as last time. It almost felt like if I used enough energy I could break free from it, but I wouldn't waste my juice until a good opportunity to escape presented itself. I needed to be smart about this. Best to let her think I had no defenses against her.

Kade! I had been trying not to think about my mate. The moment my mind flittered toward him, I started to lose control of my calm. If I lost it too badly, I would have no chance of getting out of here. Still, even knowing this, a part of me couldn't help but call out for him. *Kade!* I tried again, but there was no answer.

A small portion of the panic I had been keeping contained seeped out. My limbs were trembling and I had to remind myself how strong and capable Kade was. He would be okay. I had to believe that or my mind would be shattered and that would help no one.

"We need to talk. Shift back now."

The queen's words were commanding, each laced with mecca. But I was a queen too, and I took orders from no one. Time to show her who she was dealing with. Shaking off her icy spell, I lunged at the bars, my muzzle able to fit through as I snapped at her. One of the guards went to pull her back, but she gave him a look and he refrained from stepping any closer.

"I do not fear this rabid beast," the queen murmured. "But she will learn to fear me."

With that she turned and walked away, only pausing to call over her shoulder. "I need her willing to talk, which means you need to show her our methods of enticing prisoners to cooperate."

I knew what that meant. The Red Queen had been my aunt after all. I didn't care though. I was strong enough to withstand whatever torture they threw at me. She obviously wanted me alive, so I could fight as long as I needed to. Plus, I was too busy being grateful that she didn't seem to know about the bond between Kade and me. My mate was the only thing she could use against me right now.

The two guards followed her out, and many moments passed in silence. I was just beginning to think the winter queen was all talk when I heard boots clomping on the stone floor. An unfamiliar male fae carrying a wooden case approached my cell, flanked by two others. One was a tall and gangly female magic born with a crooked nose; she had the white coloring, unlike the last I'd encountered. The other was a short, stocky man. He had dark, angry eyes, and just a quick glance gave me shivers down my spine and had my wolf pelt standing on end. There was evil in his eyes, pure evil. The three opened the cell door and approached me. With a growl I backed my wolf up to the wall and bent low, ready to attack.

The magic born raised her hands and before I could move, she shouted, "Shift!" She then threw some type of purple powder at my wolf.

With a sneeze, my body contorted and I was suddenly being forced through the change, into my human form. The pain was almost unbearable as my body and wolf fought the magic. I wanted to howl and cry, but I wouldn't give them the satisfaction. *How was this even possible?* I had never seen anyone force a shifter to change before. What the heck was in that purple dust? Scattered around me was its glittery remains, shimmering across the floor.

The color was familiar, and the shine also reminded me of my crown.

Wait a freaking minute. It wasn't dust ... it was ground up mecca stone. No wonder it was so powerful. They literally had mecca energy in powder form. It would make any spell a thousand times stronger. Still, I could barely touch the stone in the royal estate back home. Its power was immeasurable, so how had they turned one into a weapon?

The pain eventually faded away as I lay upon the freezing and filthy stone floor. I was naked, without weapons, and at my most vulnerable, but that wouldn't stop me from fighting. I jumped to my feet, fists clenched at my sides, legs somewhat steady, staring the three down.

"You can't break me," I said, my voice quiet. I would show no emotion. That was what they wanted from me, and there was no way in hell I was giving their queen anything she wanted.

"Get dressed," the magic born ordered.

As much as I wanted to defy her for the sake of defying her, I was freezing. The cold would tire me faster and I needed all my strength. I dressed quickly, keeping my eyes firmly locked on them. The man opened his wooden case. The dull sconces of light that were scattered up high above our heads caught the glint of sharp tools. I didn't react, but on the inside I was rolling my eyes. *Seriously?*

I was a queen. Did they think cutting off my pinky would make me cry for my mommy? They were in for a surprise. I'd been trained to withstand this sort of punishment since I was sixteen. Heirs had a lot of luxury, but we also had to deal with some very painful training. If a queen were ever taken prisoner, we were to choose death over giving up any intel about our kind. Kade would be fine, Finn was safe, and Violet was on her way to healing. I could die now and it would be okay. My people were okay.

Finn! I had briefly forgotten one small point – my familiar was my literal soulmate. I couldn't die, because Finn would die. Which meant I had to be strong enough to survive this and hope that I either figured a way out, or someone came for me.

It was weird that I hadn't heard from him since I woke up. *Finn...*

Nothing happened. I felt a fuzzy reply but couldn't read it, just like when I'd tried to contact

Kade. Whatever magic was around, it was shorting out my bonded soulmates.

Taking a step forward, I was going to try my best to knock out the magic born. Without her, they would be weakened and I'd have a decent shot at escape. But before I could launch myself at her, the evil eyed man stepped in closer to me and pulled out a long, thin knife. I hesitated, unsure if he was about to attack or not. Instead, he reached down and picked up a dark block-like object and began to sharpen the blade upon it. The magic born and other guard – who I was starting to think was just here to carry the heavy torture device case – stepped back toward the entrance.

They bowed their heads, and I had a terrible feeling I knew what that meant. Sure enough, I heard the footsteps moments before the winter queen stepped into the cell, ignoring her genuflecting minions as she sort of stumbled closer to me. I was wondering what was wrong with her, when I noticed the child she was dragging behind her. *Oh crap!*

My chest clenched as the little girl, no more than five years old, fell to the floor in front of the queen. She was crying, the queen having a firm grasp of her long ponytail, her tiny pointed ears visible, huge blue eyes staring straight at me. This was so much worse than I had expected.

They weren't going to cut me. Nope, this torture was going to be of the heart and soul variety. They were going to hurt this random innocent girl and hope I wasn't a typical leader, which unfortunately I wasn't. I'd never been a big fan of sacrificing the one for the many, especially when that one was a child. A child that painfully reminded me of my little sister.

The queen dragged her even closer and I lifted my head to meet her cold dark gaze head on, letting some of my anger filter out. "You're unfit to be a leader. A true queen protects her people, they do not use them in whatever sick game you're playing. You will burn in the eternal fires of hell."

Her minions flinched at my condemnation, and I knew that this wasn't the first time Queen Crazy had hurt her people. But they didn't move or say anything. They knew better.

The queen grinned. "Do you know why you couldn't hold on to your crown, Arianna? You're weak. A true queen knows she has to do everything in her power to get the job done. In the end, I sacrifice a few for the many." Exactly what I had thought previously.

The little girl was squirming now, tears tracing down her cheeks as she tried in vain to pull from the winter queen's grasp.

"Let her go," I said, utilizing every ounce of mecca energy inside of me, trying to force her to obey me.

The man holding the knife starting grinding it even louder on the sharpening stone, making that nail grating sound.

The queen had to raise her voice to be heard over him, but she didn't reprimand him. "I will let her go. You just need to do one thing for me first. Transfer that power you stole back to me."

I laughed. I couldn't help it. "My essence? The power which was stolen from me, you mean? What makes you think I even know how to give it back? It's part of me, my soul. How does one cut out part of their soul?"

Her face, which had been calm and genial except for her crazy eyes, suddenly turned cloudy and dark. Icy winds slammed against the walls. "That's not my problem. You need to figure it out ... and fast."

She turned to the man holding the knife. "Cut her," she said, as she casually tossed the girl at him.

Dropping the stone, he caught her in one swift movement, his huge hand wrapping around her tiny throat. Without pause, he brought the blade to the girl's forehead. That's when I lunged for him. Halfway to him, a blast of frigid air hit me and I was slammed back into the wall. I looked up at the ice queen and threw my own blast of mecca her way, but she easily deflected it.

The girl shrieked and I watched in horror at the man sliced a small gash in her forehead.

"Stop! Okay! I'll do it! Just stop." I placed my hands up, never taking my eyes from the child. She would not be hurt any more because of me.

The queen seemed satisfied, giving me a little smirk. I calmed my expression so that I didn't bring any attitude with my words. "I wasn't lying when I said I don't know how to do this, but I have an idea. I will need a night to think on it."

Total lie. I had no freaking clue, but I needed to buy some time.

The queen's smirk morphed into a glare that took over her entire face. She started scanning my body, as if she could figure out if I was telling her the truth. "What way do you think you know?"

I stood frozen for a moment, and then blurted out the first thing I could think of.

"The mecca crystals. I think the power could be transferred through one." I hoped to God it wasn't true, because that meant giving this evil woman part of my soul, but ... I couldn't stand to see this innocent little girl suffer for me.

That seemed to satisfy the queen, because she nodded to the tall man carrying the case. "Keep the girl overnight in case Arianna suddenly forgets her idea by morning."

The magic born was glaring at me, and I hoped she didn't have the power to read minds, because the only thought I was having was how to break out of here and find Kade. After a tense pause, the magic born nodded and they all disbanded. Tall man carried out the case and the girl, but the stocky man stayed. He still had his blade.

He pulled up a chair and sat right in front of my cell. A low headache started to throb at my temples as I listened to their retreating steps. What the hell was I going to do? This new power inside of me was shooting around like a live wire, and I had no idea how to use it. It felt like my mecca power, but also different, like it was angry and needed an outlet. Which made me hesitant to tap into it. I'd had problems with new powers and the mecca in the past, and this time Kade wasn't here to help me.

Knifey reached down to a pile of wood at his feet, grabbed a piece, and then using his knife started whittling away like he didn't have a care in the world. I slid down and just sat there, going over all of my options. My best chance was in taking this guy out, hoping he had a key on him, and escaping. Or alternatively, taking him out, and if he didn't have a key, then taking his knife so I would at least have a fighting chance over the next people to open my cell. I'd wait for him to lose some focus though. Right now he was definitely on guard. Even though he was feigning disinterest, he was keeping a firm eye on me.

With the magic born gone, I attempted to contact Finn and Kade again, utilizing more and more mecca power as I tried to project my voice. Nothing. They'd better be okay. I would know if either of them were dead, but otherwise there was no way I could tell their condition. Not blocked like this.

After an hour of sitting in complete silence, footsteps broke the stillness. Knifey didn't turn his head, but I was immediately tensed, preparing myself. So far there had been no welcomed visitors to my cell, and something told me this time would be no different.

A tall and regal looking man, around his mid-thirties in age, turned the corner, and as I got a clear view of him my stomach knotted. His long white-blond hair was braided at the sides, fae ears sticking out. But what had me frozen to the spot were his eyes. The very same shade of turquoise had stared back at me in the mirror my entire life. The high-born fae was silent as we took a moment to stare at one another. The moment I realized who he was, I stood slowly. I would not be looked down upon by him.

He might be my biological father, but he was no family of mine.

He pressed himself closer to the bars, like he couldn't help but close the distance between us. His scent wafted toward me and it was familiar, a smell that had my wolf howling deep inside of me. It was the floral fragrance that had been in the Red Queen's library the night she died. Rage built in my chest as I clenched my fists at my side, fighting down the shift. My words were low, laced with every ounce of hatred I could muster.

"You're a murderer. You killed her, didn't you?"

His voice was light and airy, not at all what I expected. I was used to the gruff tones of shifters – especially Kade. This fae's voice was almost wispy, weak.

"Who? Rosalina? Of course I did. It was my duty to end that traitor's life."

His blatant admission caught me off guard, but if he was in a sharing mood, I wanted to know everything. He was my enemy, and information might help me escape.

"Why would you kill the Red Queen?"

He looked at me as if I were pathetic, sneering with a curled upper lip. Dammit, he looked so much like me. It was disconcerting and I kind of wanted to rearrange his face.

After all of this posturing, he finally said, "I expected more brains from someone like you. Your lineage is ... outstanding. I guess breeding doesn't always win out."

He was seriously overestimating his lineage, that was for sure. Before I clued him in on this, he continued: "I murdered that betraying waste of monarchy because the Red Queen was your mother. She hid your existence from me, which she should never have done, so I had to end her."

Blackness crept in at the edges of my vision as his confession reverberated through my mind. The Red Queen ... my mother. *No!* No, that couldn't be. She had never carried a child to full term...

My breathing was coming in and out in short bursts as I fought to control my emotions. The power inside of me was spiraling out of control, but now was not the time to lose it. I needed to know more.

"So the Red Queen was my mother, and you're my father ... how? Tell me how this all happened!"

My attempt to contain my emotions was not going well. I had to curl over on myself to stop the wolf bursting free. As I leaned forward I caught a glimpse of knife guy. He had abandoned all pretense of whittling and was staring wide-eyed at me. No idea what he had to be so shocked about. This was my life out of control here.

Once my wolf was locked down again, I straightened, and standing as tall as I could, let my gaze rest on Luca. That was what Violet had called him, right? I refused to give him a title, either familial or royal. He had his head tilted to the side, the slightest smirk on his face, relishing in my shock and discomfort. He was enjoying telling this story. I wished I could just tell him to screw himself, but I needed to know. Not just for myself, but for all of my people who were suffering from the Red Queen's actions.

But one thing was for sure, I would give him no more satisfaction with my emotional turmoil. I schooled my face, showing him only what I wanted to. Cold eyes, hard features.

He faltered for a moment before continuing his story: "Twenty years ago, Earth time, I was working as a liaison for my mother. We wanted to control the mecca power on the Earth side, and to do so we needed to form a relationship with the shifter king or queen. The bear king was an untrusting and wily sort of man, tough to crack, so we started with the wolf queen."

Those turquoise eyes went a bit misty, the way mine did when I was reliving pleasant memories. At one point or another he had liked the Red Queen, but clearly not enough to spare her life.

"Anyway, she was guarded at first, but soon became open to an alliance between her court and the Winter Court."

"You seduced her," I said, cutting through his bullshit.

He laughed, and I fought the urge to cross the room and yank the knife away from evil-eyes so I could stab this horrible fae to death.

"Yes, it was one of my easier and more pleasant assignments. We carried on an affair for some time. I was mostly in the Otherworld, but we could communicate through the flowers, and I would come across to meet up with her. We had plans to take out the bears. That way she would control all the boroughs, and then I would control her."

The flower in her personal items. The picture of her pregnant with her sister – the shifter I had always believed to be my mother. The Red Queen was not the one who miscarried, it must have been my mother. Or more correctly my aunt.

"So then what happened?"

Clearly they hadn't taken on the bears, and the fae had left us alone for twenty years after I was born. There had been no trouble until the night the queen was murdered. So what went so terribly wrong after all of those years?

The prince's face darkened then, his emotions simmering closer to the surface. Maybe he would be the one to lose control. Maybe I could take advantage of that.

"One day she stopped calling for me, and would not answer my summons. When I tried to see her, she refused to come to our meeting place. My mother decided that we should let it cool down, and that the basis I'd formed was still good for an alliance, but I knew something was going on. Against my mother's orders, I snuck into Rosalina's private quarters and found her pregnant. She told me it wasn't mine, and I believed her. She had other lovers, and fae cannot breed with shifters. Still..."

He trailed off, that wistful look back on his face. "I couldn't let it go then. In the past, if a fae and Earthsider bred together, something crazy always came from it. Like when the fae and humans bred together so long ago ... we got shifters. And if any fae was strong enough to overcome previous infertilies, it was me. I went to my mother, told her what I discovered. She was worried that if this child was mine, conceived with the queen of the shifters and basically born of two leaders filled with mecca, it could be powerful enough to take over everything.

"So I waited, and when Rosalina gave birth, I snuck back to Earth, only to find her mourning a dead shifter child. She held the still bundle in her arms, cried over it, and … I knew we had nothing to worry about."

Cold bastard. That must have been my cousin. The Red Queen had switched babies with her sister, thereby making sure no one knew her child had survived. Her child with a fae. *Me.* My head was reeling.

"She hid you from me!" The arrogant fae was angry, his cool façade fading away. "Stole your fae essence with the help of magic born and passed off a dead young as her own."

I'd never particularly known or liked the Red Queen. I would never have guessed she'd carried and birthed me. Even when she'd simply been my aunt, I'd never felt a bond. But I did know one thing, she had done everything in her power to protect me from this man.

"So how did you find out?"

I knew he was only freely divulging this information because they planned to kill me soon – good luck with that. They had no idea how hard I would fight to stay alive to get back to Kade and Finn, to my people.

Luca's face was blank again, emotions suppressed back into that dark cavity in his chest where his heart should be. "I let her be for a long time. We still hoped to utilize the alliance I had been forming. When the bear king died, I knew it was time to start planning for a revisit. His people would be vulnerable with a new king. So after some time I surprised her with a visit. She was in her library and didn't smell me coming. She had your fae essence locked in the container, and the moment I saw it, felt the familiar energy, I knew what had happened. She must have spelled you at birth, locked away the fae part of you so I would never sense you if I visited Earth. She had it all planned."

"So you killed her and took my essence. Why didn't your queen just break the jar like I did?"

He shook his head. "It's your essence. You're the only one who could release it and gift it to another."

So many questions were answered now, but still I had a million more. "If you wanted my essence, why did you try and have me killed on the night of the queen's death? You sent a hit out on all the vortexes. If I was dead you'd never get your essence."

"I panicked. I had no idea what I had created, and I had no idea which of the heirs you were. At that point we thought our magic born could release the essence, so we didn't need you."

"So you just want my power?"

My entire life, a very small part of me had yearned for my father, to know him, to wonder if he would care more than my mother had. I didn't exactly expect he would try to kill me the moment he found out I was alive. I mean ... wasn't that nature? Don't kill your offspring?

He sneered. "I want my mother to have your power so we can take over the New York City mecca. She has promised that on that side of the veil I can reign supreme."

Ah, that made sense. Mommy was promising him his own little kingdom to rule on the Earth side while she ruled the Otherworld. How cute. I was totally going to kill them both now.

I had to play this smart. As long as they thought I could and would give up my fae essence power, I could buy time.

"And the shifters in New York City?"

He shrugged. "The ones who survive can be of use to me somehow, I'm sure. I'll need servants of course."

I had to swallow hard to bite down the growl that wanted to rip from my throat.

"And if I transfer the magic, your mother will let me go? I'm not queen of the mecca anymore. I just want to get my friends and go. You'll never see me again."

I knew from the treeling that fae were incapable of lying, but they were very good at half-truths. He gave me a pitiful smile. "Transfer the magic and we'll let you out of here."

Hah. Clever. Let me out of this jail cell and then kill me. I pretended to be entranced by his promise, nodding lightly.

He seemed pleased. "Good girl. Now figure out how to transfer that power by morning or you and that child will both be in a world of pain."

This time I couldn't stop the growl from ripping from my throat. Bastard. He had said his piece – had his two minutes to brag about his role in everything – and now he turned his back on me and spoke to the guard.

"If she does anything suspicious, you know what to do," Luca said. The man whittling his wood simply nodded, letting the light catch his blade.

I knew I could take this guard one on one, but if he alerted the others I would be in trouble. Without another word, the pale-haired fae spun on his heels and walked away. He didn't look back once. Meanwhile I was in a mild panic. I needed to figure this out, needed to escape immediately. I had no idea where Kade was. Why couldn't I talk to him or Finn? How the hell was I going to get out of here?

I was so screwed.

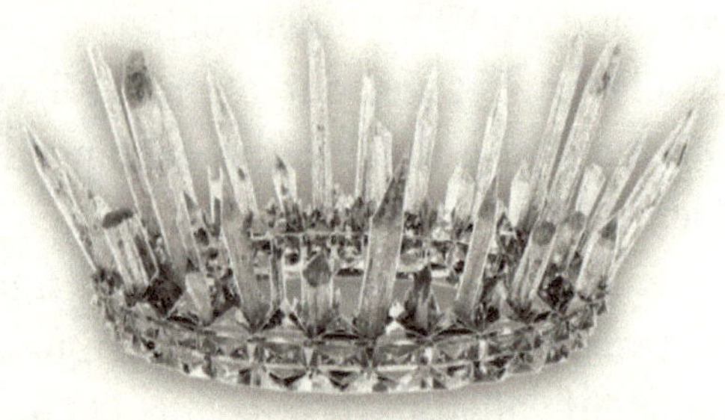

Chapter Nine

Freedom always has a price.

OVER THE NEXT two hours I waited for a sign that the guard was tiring or losing focus. It had to be nearing the middle of the night now. But the stubborn bastard just kept whittling away like he was hooked up to a coffee IV.

I decided to test the waters. "I'm thirsty."

If I could get him to come closer, I could lash out with mecca through the bars and hopefully knock him out close enough to reach his keys.

"You'll live," he replied curtly and kept whittling. Argh! I decided the best thing I could do would be to fake sleep. Curling up on the straw mat, I faced the wall and stared out of the little drain grate there. Inside of it, I could see a few frozen blades of grass, so I focused on them for over an hour, all the while pinching my inner thigh to keep myself from dozing off. I could not fall asleep first. Eventually, he would move, drift off, or pee. Right?

As my patience waned, I decided I would give it only a little longer, and then I would just lash out with mecca anyway. I'd have to use more if he was alert, hit him really hard. Hopefully the power wouldn't get out of control and kill me.

A shadow moved in front of the drain grate then and I froze, blinking a few times as I waited to see what was entering the hole. *What in the...?* A large tan hand passed in front of the rectangular grate and I had to force myself not to move. If the guard was watching me, I still wanted him to think I was asleep. The hand passed a small paper note through the grate bars and held it there in midair, one tip of the finger poking it through the bars. My heart nearly stopped beating as I reached out slowly, keeping my back stiff to the guard, and took the note. I let my fingers graze against the other hand, so the person knew I was alive. Clearly this drain led to the outside world, and had thankfully been just large enough for the male to shove his note through. In a flash the hand was gone, and the frozen blades of grass became my only view again.

It was dark in the cell but not pitch black. The lights in the hallway outside my cell still shone. Slowly I unrolled the note and glanced down at it. I was relieved to see it was written in English, a rough masculine scrawl.

I'm Kade's brother. I saw where they took him and I'm going to free him. My wife is waiting by the eastern gate where her brother is a guard. She has a horse for you and Kade. Break out and get there and you can be free. She can only wait until first light, then the changing of the guard happens.
Be well.
Kian

My heart was pounding in my throat as I gingerly folded the parchment and tucked it into my bra for safe keeping. Holy ... *holy* crap! I had been right, Kade's brother had been living in the Otherworld this entire time. He had a wife and child. My mind was reeling.

I wasn't sure if fae could sense heartbeats, so I closed my eyes for a few moments and just breathed to settle myself. Meditation always calmed me, so I drew on that training, and let my essence flow free, just enough to have my heart steady again and my mind relaxed. Well, some of it. The other part was mentally rereading that note.

Kade's brother was on his way to rescue him, and I had an escape plan. This changed everything. I said a silent prayer then: *Dear Universe, when I roll over, please let this man be asleep. Double please.*

Ever so slowly, I craned my neck.

Mutha—

He was still cutting that stupid piece of wood. He seemed really into it though, because he didn't notice I had moved. I slowly rolled my head back and stared at the wall. Okay, time for a new plan. I was proficient enough with mecca now that I was pretty sure I could manipulate the door lock – well, enough that I would be able to get out of this cell. Of course, then I would have to use more mecca to take out the whittler, and that might be too much channeling of energy in one day. Without Kade here to filter the mecca if it began to drown me, I could end up passed out or dead. I needed to conserve it and play this smart. Just when I had resolved myself to try using too much mecca, the man spoke.

"Girlie! You awake?"

I kept my breathing calm and even, feigning a deep sleep. Another few moments passed and then I heard rustling and the sound of retreating footsteps. The universe had just answered my call. I assumed he went to the bathroom, which meant there wasn't a moment to waste. Flipping over I scanned the hall outside my cell and saw that he was indeed gone. As I popped up to my feet I was already calling the mecca to me. My hands warmed, and that intense new power inside of me flared to life.

Crossing the cell in a few swift steps, I held my hands over the lock, blasting it with power, purple sparks shooting out like a firework show. The metal immediately grew hot, changing from rusty brown to a deep glowing red. After a few moments, I cut off the mecca power and stepped back. With one hard kick the door burst open. *Thank mecca.* I was even more relieved that so far I didn't have a headache from the use of my power.

First order of business, I needed a weapon and a disguise. Stepping out of the room I took a left, the same way the wood whittler had gone, the way out. I passed half a dozen cells, trying my best not to look into them. I wanted to save everyone here, but in doing so I would probably not escape myself. And then the other little girl would die. It was a hard choice, one I hated to make. Hopefully I'd figure out a way to help the prisoners of the winter queen.

I paused as I passed a small alcove. Maybe my luck was looking up, because nestled above the small outcropping of stone there was a sickle. The curved blade was large, the handle ornately carved from what looked like bone. It was a macabre display though, dried blood remained across the blade, but that was okay. It was a weapon.

Pulling it from the wall, I was surprised to see a glint of sharp steel shining under the grime. I wasn't an expert or anything, but I was thinking this might be elven made. *Perfect!* Turning, I padded down the hall, before the sound of footsteps had me freezing and shrinking back into a small curved section of wall.

As the footsteps got louder, I raised the sickle and prepared to fight. I would not go back into that cage, I would not risk the life of a little girl. The whittler went by my alcove. He was stumbling a little, barely paying attention. He was almost passed, and I was just congratulating myself on the third piece of luck for the night, when he must have caught sight of me in his peripherals.

As he turned to better see inside the alcove, I leapt out. As much as I had the element of surprise, he was well trained and already prepared for the attack. His arm came up to protect his head and the sickle sank into the meat of his forearm with a thud. He grimaced and groaned, shooting out with his other arm, cracking me in the shoulder. I pulled the sickle back quickly and pivoted out of his reach. I had limited mobility in the confines of the hall, but there was enough room for now.

When he came for me again, I feigned left and he took the bait, shifting his weight that way. He was strong and well trained, but speed was not his strength. With that in mind, I switched directions, and using every ounce of my wolf prowess, slammed the sickle into his neck, cutting halfway through, and he fell to his knees, gurgling. Not one for prolonged and painful deaths, I shoved the sickle further in and ended him.

Dragging his limp body into the alcove, I quickly searched him, taking a ring of keys and his sword, leaving the sickle behind. I would have loved his jacket but it was covered in blood. I would have to find another disguise. Stepping back out into the hallway, I came face to face with a prisoner, a very tall, dirty-blond, male fae. He had the high aristocratic features that I associated with royalty in this world, his eyes a mix of blues and greens.

He was up against his cell bars, those stunning eyes wide, having watched what I had just done. He was wearing an ankle-length warm-gray woolen cloak. I held out the keys in my hand.

"Give me your cloak and I'll give you the keys. Just promise me that you will wait one hour to escape, and you will free every other innocent prisoner in here."

He was a highborn fae, and my nose told me he was from the Summer Court. Somehow I could detect the slightest difference in the floral scent. I hoped he would know who was innocent and who wasn't in this hellhole.

"I promise I will do exactly as you've asked. You have my word," he said as he ripped his cloak off and shoved it through the bars.

As I grabbed the warm garment, I dropped the keys at his feet. "There's a slave entrance that leads to the woods. It's only guarded by one man," I whispered. "That's your best way out. Don't leave any children behind."

He gave me a nod, and returned my whisper, "They will be safe in the Summer Court." I had been right. Looked like I was slowly connecting to the fae side of myself.

He reached down and snagged the keys, tucking them deep in his pants. I turned to leave, before pausing to say, "Oh, and the queen was planning on using a little girl as leverage against me. She's about five or six, and they cut her face." I pointed to the spot on my own forehead. "If you see her at any point, please take her with you."

He nodded again, but spoke no more. I had a good gut instinct about people, and my gut was saying to trust him. Slipping the cloak over my shoulders, sword on my hip, I ran the rest of the way down the hall to my freedom.

I'm coming for you, Kade.

I made it through the castle and out into the courtyard without seeing anyone. I had been lucky. It was nighttime and it seemed only a minimum staff were around. Most of those were servants, and they were neither observant or trained in detecting escaped prisoners. No alert had sounded, which meant the guard had not been discovered yet, but I knew I was on borrowed time.

The moment I was free of the castle grounds, I called out for Finn and Kade. There was a flicker of something at the end of our bond, but neither of them responded, which freaked me out. Of course, there was no time for any sort of breakdown – and I was long overdue for one – so I decided to stick with the plan and hopefully everything would work out. The winter queen must have done something to me when I was passed out, blocked or suppressed communication of my bonded mates. Or maybe the magic born blanketed the entire city. Either way, I was on my own, which wasn't ideal, but I would trust in Kian.

Speaking of, his note had said that he would rescue Kade and that I needed to meet his wife with the getaway cart. With that in mind, I headed east, slipping my way through the shadows of the winter village. Even though it was quite dark, just a few lit fires on poles, I had no problem seeing obstacles in my path. I was used to having great vision, but this was even better than usual. I was changed, no doubt about it, so I needed to learn how to utilize my new skills. I needed to speak with a fae, preferably one who wasn't stark raving mad, and find out what exactly I should expect from this new energy inside of me.

When I figured I was about halfway to the gate, I had to hide behind some carts as a bunch of drunk men stumbled out of a tavern-looking building. It was more than a little frustrating hiding like a rat in the straw, but it was the best solution for now. Taking on a dozen idiots would be cathartic, but I had no time for that.

As the last male emerged, and the door slammed shut, I was preparing myself to start moving again when I caught sight of a familiar face. *Shit!* It was Kian, and he looked absolutely wasted as he slung an arm around a dirty looking ogre. Everything in my world went a little red around the edges then. I had to fight my wolf with more effort than ever before to stop her shifting and attacking the bear. His note had said he was going to free Kade, so what was he doing here, drunk, cozying up to the fae?

Had he already rescued Kade and this was a distraction? Or had the entire thing been some sort of setup to get me to leave without my mate. Either way, I couldn't risk it.

Kade! I tried again, my mind pushing and searching. But again, nothing. With an almost inaudible sigh, I followed the drunken fae, all of them laughing and singing through the streets. They were slow, so it was very easy to stay with them and not leave the cover of the shadows. I kept my eyes locked firmly on Kian. The moment he was alone, I was going to show him that it was unwise to mess with a wolf. Especially one who was missing her bonded mate.

One by one, the fae stumbled into their homes. It was like a drop-off service, but the slow and on foot kind. Eventually there was only Kian and the ogre left, and I had reached the end of my very limited-to-begin-with patience. I did a few quick steps and slipped in behind a bushy garden, about three feet from the pair. They had stopped right in the middle of the cobbled street. Kian started to speak and my heart literally ached at the sound. He sounded so much like Kade – that deep rumbly gruffness that sent chills up my spine.

"Come on, Ollie, you promised me you'd sneak me into the fights. You know I've never been before."

The ogre threw back his huge ugly head and laughed voraciously. "You outsider. You not allowed in. But since you drink me under the table, tonight you will get the chance."

I had a pretty good view of Kian's face then, a wash of moonlight illuminating the street. And even though he was still swaying, his dark eyes were stone cold sober. *Okay.* There was definitely more going on here, and now I was wondering if I should have just followed his note from the start.

It felt too late to turn back now, so when the ogre swept Kian along the path, they had a shadow. The pair moved much faster now, heading toward a very dark section of the village. No fires burned here, and the houses looked much more derelict. Some of them were nothing more than shells and clearly no one lived in them. If this were New York, we would be moving into the poorer and much rougher areas, where illegal activities transpired on every street corner, and even more hidden away in the underground.

The ogre and Kian stopped again, right out front of an old, rickety looking fence. I dived behind some broken timber as both of them scanned the area, then lifted up some of the fencing and crawled under. I gave them a few seconds to move before I followed, finding the tear in the chain easily and sliding under. The cloak protected me pretty well; the few scratches I got were not important. I could barely see the large shadows of the men now, so I hurried across the uneven and rocky ground, trying my best not to stumble in the dark. I got close enough to see the ogre lift a panel on what looked like a broken-down warehouse, then they disappeared inside.

In normal circumstances, I would have hesitated to follow. It was the perfect ambush situation and I had no idea if they knew I was behind them. But trusting my gut again, I believed Kade's brother was on our side. With that in mind, I found myself lifting the panel and rolling in underneath as it closed. I was on my feet in a second, crouching low to prepare myself for an attack.

I found myself in a small, storage style room with a few broken tools littered around the floor. There was no one around. I could hear lots of noise now that I was inside, which was odd, because not a single sound had penetrated to the outside. I opened the door on the far wall and entered a long hall. Following the jeering and the lights, I came upon a large crowd of fae. It looked to be at least twenty deep, and I had no clear view of what they were all crowding around. From the back, I was getting a very underground fight ring vibe. The dark shadowy expressions, the shouts and catcalling, the tickets some of them seemed to be holding – not to mention bags of clinking coins being passed around. There looked to be mostly men in here, but there were women too, so I wouldn't immediately stand out.

I could no longer see Kian or the ogre, but that didn't matter, I was here for Kade, and the slight tingling of mecca on my skin had me thinking – and hoping – he was somewhere in this building. Pushing through the crowd, no one paid the slightest attention to me. All of their gazes were locked on whatever they were circled around. My heart was pounding hard, energy swirling inside of me. I was almost afraid to look into the center of the room, but I would not be a coward today. *Kade would be fine and I would help Kian get him out of here.* That was my mantra, and it was getting me through.

Once I made it through a bunch of huge, and definitely not high-fae creatures, I could finally see what had this group so enthralled. *Holy mother of shifters.* My guess had been half right, it looked like a fight ring, but not like I had imagined. The ring was more semi-circular, the far side a flat wall, and against it were five chained fae. Two of them were highborn fae, shriveled and weak looking, one was a goblin, another an ogre, and the last one I had no name for. It was frankly weird and scary looking, grotesque: two heads, multiple eyes, gray skin, and lots of tufts of hair where hair should not be.

I was just wondering why they were tied up when a huge roar started in the crowd and the clanking of doors and chains had everyone's attention shifting to the right. I turned with them, and thankfully my gasp was drowned out in a loud outcry. Two ogres talking close by caught my attention.

"Best buy Gorbon has made. He's undefeated in three fights so far. He's a monster."

They were talking about Kade. My Kade. Who was standing shirtless on the far side of the semi-circle. His hands were bound by chains as he entered, but were being removed by a three foot tall, fairy-looking creature, and then she was out of the ring in a zip, so fast the eye couldn't track her. Pressing myself even closer to the edge of the barbed wire fence, which separated the crowd from the fighters, I drank in the sight of Kade. He was wearing nothing but a pair of cutoff shorts, his chest and body shiny with sweat or oil as his large muscles trembled. His eyes were dark and shimmering as he stalked forward.

I wanted to scream, to cry out and let him know that I was here. I wanted to call forth the mecca and blast everyone in this room to pieces, but none of that would do any good. The queen and her guards would rain down on us and we would never get away. We had to remain undetected. Somehow I needed to alert Kade to my presence, and then we had to get out of here and to the eastern gate before sunrise so we could escape.

Before I could hatch any type of plan, the cuffs clanked open on the gnarly looking creature with two heads. Another blip of sparkle showed the fairy darting off again. She was insanely fast, which made sense when you considered her current occupation.

Kade...

I tried to reach him through our bond again, but nothing happened. Damn that winter queen. I really wanted to kill her.

The crowd roared. Money was being tossed about, tickets waved in the air. Finally, when the crowd settled I did the only thing I could think of. In the complete silence I pulled my hood back the tiniest bit and shouted, "Kick his ass!"

At my taunt, the crowd lost it again, cheering, pumping their fists in the air, but Kade's entire face tightened and he turned to search the crowd. I had hoped he would recognize my voice, and thankfully it looked like he had. As our eyes met, the expression on his face was a combination of relief, anger, and this softness that he only ever showed around me. I gave him a single head nod, fighting back tears. He returned my gesture, before all of those soft emotions disappeared. If I didn't know Kade, I would have feared him in that moment. He turned then to face the creature and I quickly slipped my hood back up.

The sight of me seemed to give Kade a renewed strength. He clenched his fists and advanced on the beast. The thing's two heads were swaying, grunts coming from somewhere, even though I couldn't see anything I would call a mouth. A bell dinged from behind me and Kade tipped his head back and roared. It was his bear's roar, and it made my wolf howl deep inside of me.

Chapter Ten

North, south, east, west. Which way home is the best?

I PUSHED EVEN closer to the front, knowing that if it looked like Kade was losing the fight I would call forth the mecca and blast the two-headed monster to bits, consequences be damned. The beast reared up on hidden hind legs like a horse ready to charge, and Kade wasted no time with fanciness. He just dug his feet into the ground and charged, running right at it. I knew Kade's fighting style by now, which gave me a semblance of reassurance that he would be perfectly fine, but still, as I watched my mate slam into the beast, knocking him backwards with the force of his blows, my heart was definitely in my throat.

The beast recovered quickly, striking back at Kade with one of his taloned hands, opening a gash on Kade's shoulder, but he barely flinched. He leaped forward, grabbed one of the beast's heads in his large hands, and squeezed as hard as he could, twisting it around. The beast clawed at his back but my mate didn't seem to notice. With a loud crack, the head Kade held flopped to the side. The beast lashed out, kicking the shifter off of him, and Kade slammed onto his bleeding back, sliding across the dirt floor.

Before I could panic, Kade did a kick up and was on his feet, a set of handcuff chains dangling in his hands. The crowd roared. I guess there were no rules to these fights, and you could use anything around you as a weapon. As the beast charged him, Kade tightened the chain between two hands and pivoted to the left, swinging over the beast's back and wrapping the chain around its one still-functioning throat. Kade pulled the chain taut and the beast's eyes bugged out, its face going purple. Finally, after an agonizing minute, the fae creature dropped dead to the ground and the crowd roared.

Kade was hurt. His back was bleeding and full of dirt, but he stood strong, glaring at everyone in the room, his eyes only softening when they fell on me. The next fight was quicker, and while the goblin seemed to have some healing and regenerative powers, there was nothing that could bring an opponent back from having their head and spine ripped from their body, which looked to be Kade's preferred way to end a fight. I was starting to feel positive about his odds. Only three to fight left, and then I assumed they would let him sleep or rest or whatever, and we would sneak out.

That's when the fairy girl looked at the crowd and called for them to quiet down.

"Let's make this interesting, shall we?" she yelled into the room, and the crowd went wild. I leaned forward, wondering what she was going to do. She flitted across the arena and the chains clanked off the three remaining fighters. A highborn fae man, a highborn female, and an ogre. Crap. Kade was strong, but he was injured and three against one were not odds I wanted on my mate.

The highborn woman looked the fiercest of all the fighters, outside of the guy with two-heads who was now dead. She did look a bit emaciated, but still tough. She wore all black, including a leather corset and canvas pants. Not to mention her thin arms were littered with rock hard muscle. This wasn't her first fight; she knew how to survive.

She looked up at the fairy and said, "Anything goes?"

The fairy nodded. The bell hadn't rung yet, but in one quick movement the female highborn did a roll and popped up next to Kade. My mate tensed, ready for anything, but the girl just gave him a sidelong glance and extended her hand. "Partners?"

He paused, staring her down for a beat, before a grin slowly lifted one side of his lips and he took her offered hand. She was smart, picking the strongest and partnering with him. I wondered if in the end the fairy would force them to fight one another. Something we would deal with if it happened. The moment Kade and Badass chick's hands met, the crowd roared. They liked the idea of this team up. The fairy wasted no more time now, and rang the bell to start the round.

Kade and the female highborn moved together as one, almost as if they had been fighting as a team for many years. The pair they faced looked slightly nervous, but didn't hesitate to step forward either. When there was about three feet between the four of them, Kade and his partner quickly split apart so that they could come in from either side. I had been right about this badass chick, she was trained, and fast. She had her opponent on the ground in a headlock within seconds, which left Kade to deal with the ogre.

My mate flicked one quick glance in my direction, as if he just needed to reassure himself that I was still there, that I was still safe, and then he launched himself at his massive foe. The ogre was strong but slow, which allowed Kade to get in a few heavy hits before he received one back himself into the chest. With a bearlike roar, his body started to shift into his in-between form, which gave him some of the strength and speed of his full bear form.

With both hands, he latched onto the ogre's arm and wrenched it to the right. At the same time he released his left handhold and smashed that fist into the fae's face. He then rained down as many hard and heavy blows as he could manage. The ogre got a few of his own in as well, but he was vastly outpowered by the bear king.

It didn't take long before Kade and his fae partner had the other two either knocked out cold on the ground or dead. It was hard to tell. The dirt had turned to mud with the blood, and it made my stomach twist. Bits and pieces of fae were scattered around the ring, and I wondered how many had died down there for the entertainment of others.

I knew whatever happened next would determine how we got out of here. My mate would never kill a female unless it was life or death, and he would especially not want to kill this one after they had just fought to save each other's lives. If the fairy called for them to fight each other, I was going to have to unleash the mecca and hope for the best. We would have to run, and running would probably entail the queen's guard on our heels.

My hands stilled in the air, heat burning below the surface, as the fairy took center stage, her gossamer wings flitting about.

She seemed to consider the two before her. "What do you say? Another fight?" she asked, and the crowd roared, though less than they had earlier. The fairy seemed to consider Kade and the female again. "Or shall we let them get some sleep and round up a new group tomorrow? Start two man fights from now on? That was rather fun to see."

This time the crowd's roar was deafening; the walls shook as it thundered on. All I could think was, *Thank the gods*.

Within moments, the crowd began to disperse. The fairy waved her hands, producing some magical blue chains, which were then looped around Kade and the female's hands. They were then ushered toward the back exit. I was just figuring out what to do when a heavy arm dropped around my shoulders.

I was already swiveling to fight when a familiar voice halted me. "Hey, pretty lady! Wanna go home with me?" Kian's strong voice slurred close to my ear and I saw the drunken ogre leering at us with a perverted look. He then chuckled and waved to Kian, before disappearing through the front exit with the crowd.

The moment the last of the crowd deserted the fighting area, Kian dropped his arm and his act. His next words were low and clipped. "I'm glad to see you got out, but you were supposed to meet my wife." It wasn't necessarily a scolding tone, but he sounded concerned.

I gave him a look, before saying dryly, "Would you leave your mate? Trust someone you never met to save them?"

His broad features tightened. He looked so much like Kade it was uncanny. I had no doubt that these two were brothers, despite Kian being slightly shorter and less bulky, his hair sandy brown rather than the deep rich dark brown of Kade's, his eyes a light mossy green.

He just shook his head. "No. I wouldn't." With that he charged for the door the fairy had gone through and I was right on his heels.

The fairy was either extremely powerful or far too complacent, because she was leading the two fighters out alone. I could see a cart in the distance, waiting in the shadows, which I suspected was the transport to take the fighters back to their prison. We closed in on them. Kian was almost as fast as his brother and just as stealthy as he stuck to the shadows. I remained right on his tail.

Kade! My mental shout went unheard again.

The fairy's pace really picked up, and whatever magic she was using hurried Kade and the female fae along as well, but thankfully it looked like we would reach them before they reached the cart.

I called mecca to myself. It filtered up through me, bringing with it some of my newly discovered fae powers. Still wary about what these powers would produce, I hesitated to use them in such close proximity to my mate. Still, we would have to do something quickly. Once they reached the cart, there was no knowing where they were going or what powers the fairy might have to contain them.

Kian gave me the perfect opportunity when he stepped out of the shadows and started running like a lunatic, waving his hands in the air toward the trio. He was acting a combination of drunk and crazy now, which had the fairy pausing. She even took a step away from her prisoners. This gave me the chance to aim my energy at the cuffs binding my mate and the female fae.

Please let this work. Please let this work.

I gently let the mecca trickle free. The energy glided in a beaming arc from me, and instead of being its usual rich purple color, it was now a deep luminescent midnight, as if the purple were laced through with a dark blue, topped off with some shiny sparkles. The fairy, still staring at Kian, didn't even notice as the cuffs fell away from her prisoners.

Looked like my earlier question was answered – complacent and not powerful.

I ran as fast as I could toward Kade, stumbling over the uneven ground. My eyesight was still far too good for a normal shifter, but I was moving so fast a lot of that was negated. The moment Kade was free, he started moving toward me, as if he had known I was there all along. The female fae didn't stick around. She gave the retreating bear shifter a wave of thanks, and disappeared into the shadows.

"Ari!" Kade's voice was rough as he scooped me up into his arms. I clung to him with intensity. The need I had to touch and be close to him after not knowing if he was okay was stronger than anything I'd ever experienced. Our lips touched briefly, just a single silken slide of his mouth, and then he pulled away.

"How did you get free? Do you have a plan to get out of here?" His hands still cupped my face and were partly tangled in my hair. "Who helped you?"

I swallowed hard, the words I wanted to say stuck in my throat. We had no time, the fairy would be back in seconds; Kade's brother could only do so much to keep her distracted.

"Kade, your brother is not dead." Kade went rigid as swirling fire burned in his copper eyes. I quickly added, "He helped me, and he's arranged a way out of the Winter Court for us. He's alive."

Kian let out a bellowing roar, and both Kade and I swung our gazes to find him curled over, batting his hands in the air, trying to ward off a fairy attack. Kade, who hadn't appeared to be breathing until this point, threw me over his shoulder in one swift movement and charged toward his brother.

Now, I hated being carried. Always had, even as a child. But I understood that in this moment Kade's bear was in charge, not him. He wanted to get to his brother, his newly rediscovered brother, but he would not leave me for another second. Bonded mateship was not to be messed around with, and I remembered that feeling when I couldn't talk to Kade, not knowing if he was okay. So I was not at all surprised that he was keeping me close.

Still...

"Let me down," I said, my voice just above normal decibel level. "I can walk!"

Ignoring me, Kade powered toward Kian. My mate wasn't even hearing me, entirely focused on saving his brother. He would never leave him behind in the Winter Court, not after all of these years wondering what had happened to him.

I wasn't too keen on it either. The winter queen would somehow find out he helped us and she would kill him and his family without even a second thought. I could not have their deaths on my conscience.

Kian noticed us coming to him, and with one final slap at the fairy he knocked her down to the ground, unconscious. He then turned and dashed in our direction. I couldn't see much from my position slung across my mate's shoulder, but turning to a noise behind us, there were many more large shadows coming at us from behind the cart.

Guard patrol.

"We need to get out of here now," I said.

Kade, who had ground to a halt before his brother, appeared to be stuck in some sort of shocked state. He was just standing there, staring at Kian, his hands tightly clenched around my thighs. I was relieved when he finally dropped me gently to my feet, before he leapt forward to pull Kian into a hug, his large hand coming up to grasp the back of Kian's neck.

"Brother..." I wasn't sure which one of them said it, full of so much pain and love. Maybe both of them.

Pulling back, Kian looked behind us and jerked his head to a nearby alley. "We need to get out of here."

Kade was back in control, for the most part. He reached out to grab my hand and then we were off running, following Kian through the alley, our legs pumping hard, all of us taking turns to glance back at our pursuers, making sure we were keeping a decent distance between us.

As we reached a fork in the road, Kian grabbed Kade's forearm, yanking us both down a small alley that had been partially hidden by two overhanging awnings.

"Stay close, I know a way to hopefully lose most of them. Then we just have to hope my wife, Shelley, has not been caught yet and is still waiting at the east gate."

Kade's reply was low: "Let me guess, Ari was supposed to be with Shelley right now, to meet us at the gate." There was really no need for that level of dry sarcasm. He would never have left me behind, and I sure as hell wasn't leaving him.

Kian just laughed, giving me a wink as if to say he understood. "Glad to see not much has changed with you, my brother. Extra glad to see you found a mate equal, if not greater, in power, beauty, and control."

Kade's strong hand tightened just a little. "Arianna is queen of the wolf shifters. She is the one I met when I was fifteen, and she is my bonded mate."

Kian didn't gasp. His expression didn't even change. Considering a bonded mate was nothing more than a fairy tale, literally, his reaction was quite strange. And clearly Kade felt the same way when he asked, "You don't seem surprised to hear about bonded mates, Kian."

The slightly smaller male let out a strangled chuckle. "Nothing much surprises me anymore, but especially not when it comes to a bonded mate. I know I owe you and Mother a huge apology and an explanation. I never meant to take off and not return, but my mate, *my bonded mate*, is a bear-wolf, a dual-soul fae. There was no way for us to leave and get a portal home, and my mate was indebted to the winter queen for five winters, and we didn't want to bring that trouble to Earth."

A bear-wolf fae. That was the fae which Baladar told us of in his origin story. The ones who bred with humans and produced the first shifters. They couldn't shift as we did, but their souls were bonded to bear and wolf. Together.

We were still ducking through the alleys. Kian seemed to be leading us through a huge labyrinthine race in a bid to probably confuse any followers and throw them off our scent trail.

Kade waited for a few more beats before he said, "I can't say that I'm not angry with you, Ki, but I do understand, especially now." His hand ran up the side of my arm. "I would go anywhere and do anything for Arianna. I would expect no less from you and your mate."

Before anything else could be said, we were out of the alleyways, and the boys quieted down as we dashed through the streets of the Winter Court. From my brief time here I had a fairly good idea where we were – on one of the main paths, not too far from the eastern gate. It was lit with a few of those fire sticks, which meant we were more visible than we had been for most of our escape. This was the point we were vulnerable. We had to hurry it up.

As if I had conjured them from thought alone, a bunch of fae soldiers stepped out onto the path. Kade and Kian skidded to a halt. I took a moment to be grateful I wasn't in this alone – and two burly bear brothers were not bad sidekicks to have.

Without giving it a moment's thought, I shot out with mecca, drawing on every ounce of power I had left.

"Arianna…"

Kade was warning me, and for good reason. When I threw mecca like this without gathering it into a small ball first, it became like a runaway freight train, one my body wasn't strong enough to handle. But frankly I was more than sick of being in the Winter Court, and I would never go back to my … my grandmother's tender care, especially when she knew my weakness. She could use children and the innocent against me. Not today.

My hands were lit up like the aurora borealis. Swirls of midnight blue and deep purple continued pouring from my fingertips, and Kian actually took a step back. Smart man. The fae soldiers attacked and I moved my aim to hit them directly with mecca fire. And holy shifter babies, my original mecca energy was completely attached to the fae power now. Together they were more powerful than anything I had ever seen or felt before. And I didn't hold back, knowing Kade was here to save me if I went too far.

After a few direct hits of power, the guards were disabled, and thankfully I had no trouble cutting off the energy, locking it back inside.

Stepping forward, I surveyed the men on the ground. Most were unconscious, still breathing, but a few had blood dripping down from their noses.

"Sweet winter mercy," Kian muttered.

Kade was all up in my face then, raising his hands to my head. "How do you feel?"

It was then I realized I didn't have a headache. In fact I felt energized, better than I had two minutes ago, as if calling up this fae power had *healed* me.

Kade scanned my face and body, his furrowed brows smoothing out as he realized I was fine. Lowering his hands, he stepped back, and looked a combination of intrigued and confused.

"Come on." Kian jerked his head and we followed him, ready to leave this hellhole behind forever.

At the east gate, I was relieved to see only two guards and a woman with a horse-drawn cart waiting there. This gate was smaller than the main entrance, just a door inside of a fence really, clearly not a heavily used entrance. As we approached, the guards kept their heads up, looking past us as if they didn't even see us. Whatever Shelley had done, it was working. They were just going to let us through.

Kian rushed to his wife, who was at least six foot tall and willowy, with long cascading tresses of golden-red hair. Absolutely stunningly beautiful. Definitely a fae who stood out in a crowd. As they embraced, I could literally see the love between them, and I wondered if that was what Kade and I looked like now that we were bonded mates.

Kian pulled back and said in a low growl, "Nathanial?"

Shelley jerked her head toward the cart. "Asleep," she replied. I guessed Nathanial was their son.

The pair faced us, and Kade gave a small head nod to Shelley. "Thank you for all you have done to help Ari and myself. We owe you a debt of gratitude. We insist that you three come with us back to New York City."

She smiled so radiantly it lit up her already stunning face. "No thanks or debt needed, you are family. And if you can get us a portal, we will go."

"We can," I assured her, looking back at the guards, who were still standing there like none of us were nearby. Light was starting to filter through the fence, shining across their perpetually young faces. The sun was coming up. We needed to leave or risk being stuck here forever.

"My gift," Shelley said. "I can confuse people. My great, great, grandmother was a magic born."

My eyebrows lifted, eyes widening. "You confused your own brother?"

She nodded. "That way the queen will not kill him when she interrogates him."

I already liked her; she might be beautiful, but smart and caring were much more attractive.

"Let's move." Kian swung the gate wide open and Shelley nudged the horse and small cart through. As Kade and I followed, my knees almost buckled as a burst of energy caressed my body ... and then I could hear Finn yelling in my head.

Ari! My familiar sounded frantic.

I'm here! We're coming. We're all safe. Tears filled my eyes, overflowing and trailing down my cheeks. I couldn't help it, I missed my dear friend, and his voice in my head was the greatest sound in the world right now. High-pitched shrieks above me told me that Kade had signaled Nix.

Finn's tone sounded emotional when he said: *Violet is healed. Get to the campsite north of Winter Mountain. I'll find you there.*

For the second time, a surge of relief just about brought me to my knees. I had been in survival mode during my imprisonment, and at the back of my mind had been a deep-seated panic for my friends and family. I had no idea if they had escaped, if Violet had survived. I hadn't been able to think about it or I'd lose my mind and never break free, but now that I knew everyone was okay…

I crumbled.

Kade wrapped his arms around me, hauling me up and cradling me close to him, almost like a baby. I struggled for a second before realizing I needed the comfort. So, for a few moments, I let myself be hugged, let Kade take the burden of my emotions. He strode across to the cart and with no effort at all climbed in, sitting with me cradled in his lap. Kian jumped up to the bench seat, beside his mate, and then we were off.

Letting my body relax into Kade, I enjoyed our closeness as I tried to calm the tumultuous emotions crashing inside of me. It took some time, but finally I was able to speak without my voice wavering. "Where has Nix been during our capture?"

Kade's breathing got a little deeper, his voice raspy. "She attacked a few of the guards trying to find us, but then they started hunting her using magic, so she hid out for a bit, keeping herself in position should I reappear again."

"She must have been so worried not being able to communicate with you," I murmured.

His chest rumbled. "She was."

He didn't say any more. His fury of what had happened was only growing.

Deciding I'd been babied long enough, I slipped off Kade's lap to see our surroundings better. A small section of the cart, just in behind the bench that Kian and Shelley were on, was covered, and I peeked inside to see a sleeping boy bundled in a blanket. A little white rabbit was snuggled on his lap. His familiar I was guessing.

"So where am I going?" Kian asked, turning his head around to see us.

"North of Winter Mountain, to a campsite. Help is waiting," I said, and with that the horse took off and we left the Winter Court behind.

Kade was looking at the sleeping boy, emotion swimming in his amber eyes. "Is that...?" His voice was very husky.

Shelley reached back and took Kade's hand. "Nathanial, your nephew. We have told him all about you and your mother and New York. We talk about you guys every day."

Now my eyes were swimming with emotion, and Shelley took her hand off of Kade's and placed it on mine. "Thank you for coming to get us. Even if by accident. It's all I have prayed for these past five years."

I could only nod, emotion clogging my throat. My mate's brother had been found, alive and well. With a wife and child. It was sort of a miracle. And right now, we really needed all the miracles we could get.

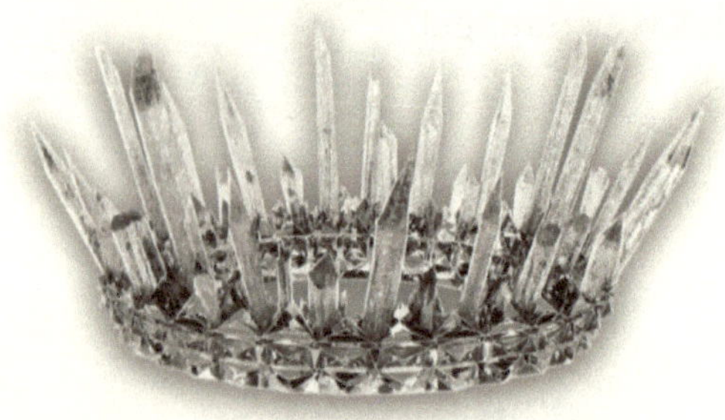

Chapter Eleven

The insidious creep of frostbite.

DURING THE FIRST twenty minutes of travel, which were thankfully uneventful, I used our bond to tell Kade everything I had learned about my bloodline and true mother. To say he was angry was an understatement.

They both deserve to lose their heads over their treatment of you. He had me wrapped up tightly against him, shielding my body with his. *The Red Queen is only slightly less guilty, because she clearly tried to protect you from the fae.*

I sighed, relishing our closeness. It had been scary being separated, taken by our enemy, not knowing if we would ever see each other again. This was a gift.

Yes, she did, but it was her fault to start with. How could she be so stupid as to begin an affair with a winter prince?

Kade stared off into the snowy distance, his warm furs tickling my cheek. *I only met her a few times, but her weaknesses were obvious from the start. Arrogance and love of power. It clearly blinded her.*

I snorted. *Yeah, she probably thought she would be the one to control him, to gain the Otherworld side of the mecca power.*

I had no doubt that both of my biological parents had started their affair in the hopes of manipulating the other. In the end though, I had ruined both plans.

Not wanting to think about it any longer, I turned my head to regard the couple up top, who were controlling the horses. I cleared my throat to break the silence, and both looked in my direction.

"I'd really love to know your story," I said. "How did you two meet? How did Kian end up in the Otherworld?" Shelley and Kian exchanged a look, and he gave his mate a nod. I felt Kade straighten beside me, and knew he was ready to hear this story too.

Shelley twisted around to see us better, her voice low and even. "My father betrayed the queen a long time ago, and it was my duty to work off the debt. The queen heard of my gift and employed me to use it on anyone she saw fit for the many years of my sentence. I confused people into seeing things that weren't there so the queen could slip in and do whatever she wanted." Fine lines formed around her eyes; her regret and pain were clear. I decided to return her earlier kind gesture, and I reached out and grasped her hand, giving it a gentle squeeze.

She continued with a wonky smile. "One day the queen said she had found a way into the Earth realm, and wanted me to confuse the bear king so she could get some information. I was scared but I agreed. She had already killed my father and was threatening to kill my mother. I felt I had no choice. A few magic born opened the portal, and as we stepped through I was amazed. The bright lights, the tall buildings!" Some of her sadness dissipated under the awe reflecting across her face. *Yep.* New York City would do that to a person, capture them and never let go. My heart ached for my home.

She swallowed hard. "I confused the king and his guards so that the queen's magic born could spell the water behind his house, to be used as a portal for future fae to enter."

Kade growled lightly at that, but Shelley, probably used to it from Kian, didn't even blink. "But something went wrong. The portal we had opened to come in wasn't closing like it was supposed to, and the winter queen left me and a magic born to deal with it as she traveled back here through the water. That's when Kian showed up. The moment I saw him I knew he was my bonded mate. Fae can tell from just one look. Everything inside of me changed that day, rearranged itself to be with him. The magic born tried to hurt him, but I killed her. Killing her caused the portal to go haywire, because she had created it. It turned into a black mass of energy and sucked Kian and I inside. Then it exploded. To this day there is still a burnt part of forest on the south edge of the winter palace."

"I wish I would have known," Kade said. "I searched for you all over the boroughs, even outside the city, but never would I have imagined you were alive and living in a mythical land."

Kian's green eyes were shiny, almost reflective as he too turned in his seat to see us better. "You could never have known, Kade, and there was nothing you could have done. Once we were in the Otherworld, there was no returning to Earth. The portals were off-limits." His jaw worked as he fought for words. "The first few weeks here were rough. Shelley hid me in a nearby village, visiting every few days to teach me the way of the fae so I could blend in. There are some outsiders here, so it's not completely uncommon, but luckily no one knew I was the bear king's son. After a year, I moved into the main winter township with Shelley. She had to stay close to the queen. Over the time we tried everything to get a portal out of here, but we never could."

"That doesn't matter," Shelley said. "We're together now and we're going home." I was surprised to hear her speak of New York as her home. Kian truly must have talked about it every day.

The conversation drifted then into topics of less intensity, nothing too serious, just basic catching up. Kade and Kian especially wanted to know everything they had missed in each other's lives.

"I'm so sorry about Dad." Kian's cheeks were tinged with red. I could see the flames in his eyes. He was angry at not being there to help his father. "I'm the oldest. It was my duty to stand by the king."

Shelley dropped her head, and that caught Kian's attention. He wrapped his arm around her, keeping his free hand on the reins of the horse. "I'm sorry, my love. I would not change the last years of our lives. It's just hard to hear of the betrayal of my father. To know I wasn't able to have his back, or Kade's."

My mate reached up to clasp his hand on his brother's shoulder. "His death was avenged, and you were protecting your family."

Kian gave him a nod, but didn't look satisfied. Kade let out a rumbling laugh. "The worst thing you did was leave me to take the crown."

I think he expected Kian to laugh, but the older bear didn't. Only the slightest of smiles crossed his lips. "You still going on about that?" His eyes flicked across to me. "Don't let Kade fool you, he was always the one better suited to rule over our people."

Through our bond I sensed that Kade was uneasy with that praise, but before anything more could be said, an icy breeze washed across the cart and my attention was back firmly on our surroundings. We'd grown a little complacent, moving rapidly through the frigid, untouched landscape. There had not been a single person, fae, or evil queen, in sight, which might have lulled us into a false sense of security. And while it was cool everywhere in the Winter Court, this breeze felt ... unnatural.

I called out to my familiar. *Finn! How far are we from the meeting point?* I sent him a series of images from the landscape around us, hoping he might have some idea of our location in proximity to his.

You're close. I'm coming in from the west and will hit you in a few minutes. Just keep heading forward. I sense the queen is on your tail, but you should beat her.

"Go!" I said with as much force as I could, my focus locked on the landscape behind us. "The queen is trailing us. Finn says we should beat her to the rescue team, but we need to pick up the pace."

Kian didn't ask me anything more, didn't question who Finn was. He let go of his wife, picked up both reins, and with a terse command the horse surged forward. Kade shifted his weight until he was crouched right on the edge of the cart, balanced there as his face started to take on bear-like characteristics. I shuffled forward too, energy swirling inside of me, my new fae vision helping as I scanned the wintery surroundings looking for pursuers.

The ice picked up and I sensed the magic in it now, the same type the queen had used to literally freeze people to the spot. "Definitely the queen," I murmured to Kade. "Her icy breath is a weapon we need to avoid."

"We're almost at the spot," Kian called out. Neither of us looked away, but I did give him a wave of acknowledgement.

Finn is incoming, I said to Kade through the bond.

I can sense him. Nix is keeping an eye out and will let me know what she finds. The queen has a fog cloaking her, which means he can't see a lot from above. He then added, *Looks like she has ten winter fae with her.*

His voice lowered as he mentioned Nix. He wanted to see his familiar as badly as I needed to see mine. It had been far too long since we had touched them and let our bond be reinforced.

Finn's huge white body came into sight then, and I found myself leaning forward in anticipation, my blood fizzing, body flushed with adrenaline. Every soft emotion possible slammed into me and I had to breathe deeply to halt another breakdown. *Come on, training, I need you now.* I was a queen, we kept our crap together, and I was at the limit of my emotional leaking for the day.

Finn sprinted in behind us, and with a graceful leap crossed the last few feet to land in the back of the cart. It gave a lurching bump, but the powerful horse soon had us flying along again. I dived over and wrapped my arms around Finn. *I missed you so much,* I said as I tangled myself as close as possible into his thick fur.

He nuzzled his snout into me and said, *Don't ever do anything like that again. You should never risk yourself, you're too important.*

A queen will always risk herself for her people, you know that.

He growled lightly, but didn't argue with me again. *My only consolation,* he finally said, *was that if you died, I would also. For I would not live in this world without you.*

It took a lot of deep breathing to keep it together then, there was so much love pouring from my familiar. Even as a small child I had known how lucky I was to have this bond. It was worth all the bad that came from being an heir. My gaze brushed across Kian and I wondered where his familiar was. He would have had one. He was supposed to be king.

"Queen on my six." Kade's warning brought mine and Finn's attention right back to the end of the cart.

My eyes narrowed on the figure in white riding atop her majestic horse. Finn growled deeply beside me and said, *There are about eighteen Summer Court soldiers just beyond the mountain. They are strong, but no match for the queen and her strongest soldiers.*

Something inside of me began to hum. Magic, my fae magic, was swirling and building, aching to be free.

Kade caught my eye as if he knew I was up to something.

"Arianna..." The way he said my name had so many emotions wrapped up in it. Love, pride, fear.

I just stood and gave him a wan smile. "I'm her only match." I was half her genetics and half of the brutal Red Queen's. The thought was scary, really. If I hadn't had the upbringing I did, I might very well have turned out to be a monster. Calista was getting a huge hug when we finally got home. She was a big part of the reason why I was who I was. Her and Winnie.

My palms tingled as the magic built up inside of me. Finn bumped my leg, asking me to get on his back. I swung a leg over the giant wolf, looking back to Kian and Shelley.

"Ride fast and hard to the mountain where the Summer Court is waiting. Kade and I will meet you there."

I knew the second I leapt off this cart, Kade would be right behind me. No sense in asking him to stay. He never would.

Kian just nodded. He was a true soldier through and through, taking orders much better than Kade. Probably why the universe definitely did not make a mistake in ensuring the younger brother became king. Soldiers were the backbone of a people, but the leader was the head and heart. We had to make the big choices, the hard choices, and we had to live with the consequences of them when we screwed up. Following orders was not one of our stronger suits.

Bones cracking beside me let me know my mate was getting into battle form. The queen was only fifty yards away and gaining, frost creeping through the forest, following in her wake. Her people were on horses, spread out in a large semi-circle behind her, and I was thankful to spot no obvious magic born amongst them.

To prepare myself for what I would have to do, I pulled up the mental image of that butcher cutting an innocent girl's face with a knife. The queen had ordered that. She was evil through and through. She had attacked and killed my people. She was not my family, she was the enemy.

A swirling galaxy of energy seeped from my palms. I held it contained as I mentally urged Finn forward, and with one leap we were off the cart and galloping over the hard-packed snow. I dug my hands into Finn's fur; riding without the harness was always tricky. Bear Kade pounded across the ground next to us, kicking up flurries of snow.

Give her all you've got, Ari. I won't let the mecca overwhelm you, Kade said, his mental words a grumble of bear sounds.

She'll get all of it and more, I replied, shooting him a brief grin before focusing back on the enemy.

The queen's beautiful face looked harsh and elemental, not even remotely human, something carved from the land and the gods. She raised her hands and blue fire began growing in her palms. I would not be weak, I would not have fear. Only I stood between her and Kade's innocent sleeping nephew, and I would not allow him to be hurt.

Raising my hands and pinching Finn's body with my thighs so I wouldn't fall, I allowed my gathered energy, the clouds of purple and indigo mecca magic, to flow from me, building it into a wall – a wall waiting for direction. My intuition told me this power was inexhaustible. As long as I could channel it, it would never die out.

I was going to bank on it, so here's hoping I wasn't wrong.

The queen closed the gap, and in a single swift motion pulled her wrists back to release her ice magic, just as I threw everything I had at her. Control had always been my weakness with mecca manipulation, but now it was almost simple to direct the energy where I wanted it to go, like everything I had been trying to achieve in my training with Kade, all of those obstacles I just couldn't get past, were gone. Now it was easy.

Maybe the entire time my mecca energy had been waiting for my fae side to be restored. Like two halves of a whole, now my magic was complete. I certainly felt stronger and more controlled. And even though I had feared my fae side, its icy energy like nothing I had ever felt before, once it mixed with the mecca ... it felt familiar again.

The queen's expression barely shifted, even as my magic advanced on her, but there might have been a slight glaze of shock in her wide eyes. My wall of magic slammed into her, knocking her clean off her horse. She thudded to the ground as five of her guards rode in behind her, each pulling their horse up so they could assist their leader.

Nix shrieked above us and Kade roared, stretching up tall on his hind legs.

They have an open portal to the Summer Court. Now is our chance, Kade growled.

The winter queen was already back on her feet, arms raised as she prepared to strike again. I was torn between taking off for the portal or staying and finishing her off. There was no doubt in my mind she would come for us again. She would never stop until she either destroyed all shifters and claimed the Earth-side mecca, or finally claimed the power inside of me that she so desperately wanted. At that thought, I heard hoof beats, and a familiar energy radiated close to my back. A sob stuck in my throat as Violet's horse came in beside me.

"Vi!"

I drank in the sight of my best friend, alive, glowing with health and power. Wearing unusual garb for her, leather pants and vest, cuffs on her biceps, and weapons strapped across her back, she had gone from Renaissance chic to badass warrior.

"Glad to see you alive, friend," she said, and her eyes shone briefly before she turned toward the queen and fury descended over her shimmering features.

Without looking my way again, she held out her hand for me, her horse and Finn keeping perfect alignment. The moment our hands locked, my energy inside went crazy, bursting out of my body before I could control the flow, filling the air with the midnight light show.

"Bring it all, Ari! Both sides of your energy!" Violet shouted over the wind whipping around us.

I nodded, calling forth everything within me. She wanted the fae and mecca power? I would give her as much as I could. The queen opened her mouth and let out a shriek like a million fingernails on a chalkboard, immediately coating the surrounding trees in ice, and I fought against my instinct to cover my ears. Instead I let go of all control over my magic; whatever restrictions I'd been imposing to keep the energy contained simply dissolved, and in a rush it took off. Violet, who felt the outpouring through our joined hands, just grinned.

If I had been the winter queen, and a magic born was looking at me like that, I might have had a moment of worry.

"Burn in hell," Violet spat, and suddenly my magic transmuted into purple fire, burning across the ground like hot lava, melting everything in its path and charging right for the queen.

Violet made two quick movements with her free hand and the fire spread out in a line as far as I could see, the flames licking up to the tops of the trees. The queen threw magic at it but nothing calmed the flames as they flared tall, like a sentinel protecting us from them. Fire and ice fought against each other, but in the end the fire could not be quenched.

"Eternal fire, eternal flame," Violet whispered, and the fire crackled with a hint of blue.

Violet let go of my hand. "Let's go," she said, turning her horse around and giving the Winter

Court her back. "That fire will burn eternal. They aren't getting through."

Holy sweet shifters. That was really amazing, and I wasn't even tired. My energy, which had calmed the moment Violet let go of me, felt full and vibrant as it swirled inside. I had no headache or backlash from the power.

As I turned Finn around, Kade started his shift back to human, jogging slowly beside us. Violet magically fashioned him some clothes and he pulled them on. Despite being in his human form, he kept pace with us as we rode hard and fast, and in only a few minutes we reached the Summer Court camp at the base of Winter Mountain.

The first thing to come into view was a bunch of soldiers standing alert around Dalia and Rowan, the magic born fae. Off to the side I could see the cart, but there was no sign of Kian or Shelley. Before I could ask about them I was distracted by a portal above the burning fire. Another pale magic born stepped into view then. She had been hidden behind the flames.

Dalia came to me as I dismounted from Finn. Her eyes roved across my newly pointed ears and fae features, but she didn't say anything about that – though I sensed she had a million questions. She wasn't the only one.

She started with a half bow. "Your Majesty, we're so pleased to see you unharmed from your time with the winter queen. Rowan and Lettie have opened this portal to the Summer Court for you – but that can be changed to your borough on Earth," she quickly added. "We would really love if you'd honor my king with a short meeting. Forge an alliance in person."

Even though she was leaving it up to me, I sensed there was a lot riding on my answer here. On the one hand, I needed to get back to my people, who were probably at war in New York. On the other hand, we needed this alliance, especially now that I had met the winter queen. She was brutal, and had been working to overthrow the shifters for many long years. My escape, and her loss of my power, would definitely tip her over the edge. Not to mention they had saved my friend's life, and for that I owed them everything.

I turned to Kade, who was waiting a few feet away. He gave me that grin of his, dimples appearing. "This is your decision to make. Do you think we will learn anything from the Summer Court which might help in our battle on Earth? In the battle which will surely be brought from Selene and the winter queen?"

He made a really good point there. My instincts were telling me I needed to meet the summer king, and thank Prince Caspien. This court could become the greatest allies we had between the two worlds and the alliance might be the tipping point in the survival of the shifters.

I turned to Dalia and bowed my head. "I would be honored to meet your king."

I sent my mate a mental message: *We won't stay long. Even though I need to learn about my fae powers, we can't risk the safety of our people. War might be happening as we speak, so for now, we just thank the king and forge this alliance.*

He nodded, and did not question me further. That level of trust and acceptance was just one of the million reasons I loved him.

Noise drew my attention then. A small group dashed up from where they must have been hidden close by. Blaine, Monica, and Victor were out in front. They rushed to my side and I gave them quick hugs. Nikoli crossed to his king, bowing first, before clasping Kade's hand in a shake. Kian and his family were a few steps behind, a yawning Nathaniel draped in the bear shifter's arms.

Addressing the group I said, "I must thank the summer king in person for his kindness. Then we will head off to New York."

They nodded in understanding, and I turned to the two magic born. "We are ready. Please hurry. We really must return to Earth as soon as possible."

They smiled, and an image of rare beauty opened up beyond the fiery portal: roses, waterfalls, summer. Somehow I could feel the warmth already, even though we were still standing in the land of ice and snow.

Lettie, the new magic born, looked at me. "The flames will not hurt you. They help keep it open."

Kian and Shelley stepped closer. Nathaniel squirmed in his father's arms and I could see the little boy was holding the rabbit tightly against his chest.

"Go on, it's safe," I said to them.

The bear shifter and his family didn't move straight away and I turned to Kade, wondering what the problem was. Before I could ask though, Kian lifted his head to the sky and Nix let out a screech – followed soon after by another screech that sounded quite a bit lighter and trill-like. A different animal?

Was there trouble? Had the queen broken past the fire? I got my answer when the flapping of wings brought Nix closer. She swooped in to land on Kade's shoulders, and despite it being difficult to read a bird's expression, I was pretty sure she looked happy. Perhaps because she was not only back with Kade, but had also found an old friend. A huge black crow followed her path and landed on Kian's shoulder. His familiar.

"We've been apart for most of the five years I was here," Kian said, his voice low and rumbly. "Couldn't take the risk that someone would see her and recognize that she was a familiar. It will be nice to have my old friend back by my side." The black crow nuzzled his neck and my heart pinched. I couldn't imagine being without Finn for that length of time.

He stepped through the portal, somehow holding his son, familiar, and mate close. My heart got a little tight ... along with my throat. It was a beautiful sight to see, a man finally safe with all of his family. Monica, Victor, and Nikoli followed straight after. Blaine refused to go with them because he said his duty was to make sure I was safe and would only go behind me.

My oldest friend looked a little haggard. My imprisonment at the Winter Court had not been a happy time for him. As if he couldn't help himself, he wrapped me up in his arms quickly, before stepping back. Clearing his throat, he said: "I missed ya, Princess." The familiar term of endearment made tears prick my eyes. Violet was also looking a tad watery-eyed as she stared between us all.

"Never thought I'd see you all again," she choked out. "I had made my peace with it. As long as the winter queen didn't get what she wanted. But ... we've been given a second chance. Let's go meet the summer king and then get back home. It's time to destroy those who tried to destroy us."

Oh yeah, Selene and Sabina were getting what was coming to them. Then we would unite our people and take on the winter fae. They were going to wish they never messed with me or my family.

Chapter Twelve

Warmth does not always equal life.

THE FAE WERE still holding the portal open, so the rest of us took a breath, joined hands, and with a final look over my shoulder at the cold and barren lands of the Winter Court, we stepped through to the land of summer.

Passing through the portal this time was quite easy. It felt like thick honey coated my skin for a moment but then it was gone. As I stepped through to join my friends, I looked about at the wonder of this new land, my mouth agape.

The trees here were so tall, almost too tall for me to see the tops of them, and they were thick with foliage and life. I could see a few parts that looked diseased, like the mecca imbalance was taking its toll, but all in all, their beauty was unsurpassed. And the scent. Oh my gods, the scent was probably the sweetest smell I had ever come across.

"What is that I smell?" I asked the summer fae who were standing with us in the forest.

Dalia smiled. "That is the scent of home. The winds of our lands, the eternal summer."

Well, there you go. Pretty much everything here smelled good, because it was just the smell of their land. I'd like to take a vacation in this land when we weren't at war. I could get used to eternal summer, especially since it wasn't hot, just pleasantly warm, like the warmth coated your skin and heated you to the very depths of your core. But I did not feel over-heated or sweaty. Magic was truly amazing.

Butterflies and the sound of waterfalls had me spinning, and on my second pass I paused at the sight of a male fae standing in a beam of sunlight between two massive flower-laden trees. *The summer king.* I had never met or seen him, I just knew that's who was standing before me. He was a few inches over six feet tall, radiating power and heat. From his golden hair, the color of a ray of sunlight, to his eyes as blue as a cloudless sky, everything about him was glowing. His skin was golden, shimmering like he had been dusted with jeweled powder. I took a step closer. Kade, my friends, and Finn right behind me.

Caspien stepped out then from wherever he had been and stood beside his father. Seeing them side by side, there was no denying they were related. They looked close in age, but the king wore his experience across his handsome features, the years he had ruled shaping him into something quite formidable, a strength that even the winter queen had not demonstrated.

He wore a red velvet cloak that trailed behind him as he approached me with a genuine smile. "Queen Arianna, it is my honor to finally meet you. I am Samson, king of the Summer Court." He bowed his head and I fell into a full curtsy. I decided not to correct him and tell him I wasn't a queen anymore. I intended to change that very soon anyway.

"Your Majesty, we are well met." My appearance was not proper for meeting a king – rags covered in blood and dirt – but he didn't seem to mind. And weirdly enough, despite his intimidating appearance, I immediately liked him.

He thrust his hand out and tipped his head to Kade. "King Kade, we are well met also."

Kade shook his hand and smiled. "Well met, Your Majesty. Thank you for everything you have done to assist us, both here and on Earth."

Movement behind the king caught my attention, and I realized that camouflaged in the trees were a dozen or more summer guards. Now that I could finally see the fae, I noticed how frail they looked. They were suffering, and I didn't know how much longer they had before the mecca loss destroyed them all. I needed to make this right.

Why was the Winter Court the least affected by the imbalance? There had been a lot of power there. And food. One would think food would still grow easier in summer ... which meant the queen had done something.

The king saw my eyes raking over his thin soldiers and he tipped his head toward a path. "Would you walk with me for a moment, King Kade and Queen Arianna?"

Kade and I didn't hesitate, nodding and stepping forward. I swiveled to give Blaine and Violet a look that said to stay put. Those two were the worst with letting me venture off on my own, but I wanted the king to know I trusted him. I wanted him to trust us as well.

As the king walked, we fell in at his side, and brushed through some overhanging plants. As I touched them a lot of the leaves crumbled into my hands. It was becoming very clear that although the plants looked green and radiant, they were dry and brittle. They were dying.

"Go ahead. Touch it." The king nodded to the plant I was inspecting. There were a few red berries left on the branch and I reached for them, inhaling sharply when they disintegrated. It was like all of the life and water had been sucked out of them but the color remained. Just like the ones I had brushed over before, the leaves crumbled to the ground.

The king watched my expression closely. "Can you fix this? Because without your help we will surely die."

I didn't hesitate, not even for a moment. "Yes, I will make this right. The mecca will find balance again."

He nodded but didn't look as hopeful as I would have liked. Something else was bothering him.

Kade pressed him. "What's on your mind?"

King Samson reached up and rubbed his temples with a small grin. "I've grown worse at hiding my stresses in my old age."

It was Prince Caspien, who had been following close by, who spoke for his father. "There is a greater evil than the winter queen, one which has been slowly seeping across the land. The loss of mecca was devastating, but it's this darkness that could finish us all completely."

I kept my eyes locked on him, waiting for the point he was trying to make. What could be worse than the winter queen?

"In the darkest parts of the Otherworld, there is a place where demons are made, a place where no life or green exists. This darkness has flourished with the loss of mecca, and ... we believe the demons might be coming for you."

The summer king jumped in: "We were attacked en masse by erchos, killans, slimers, and many others just a fortnight past. It was the reason we were not there to stop the Winter Court crossing the barrier to Earth during your summer festival. This makes us wonder if maybe the dark lands and the winter queen have formed an alliance. You need to tread very carefully, Queen Arianna. Do not find yourself in the dark lands, and beware of their ability to come to Earth."

His warning sent chills up my spine, the hairs standing up on my arms. All of the pieces were clicking into place now. "The ercho was trying to take me," I breathed, and Kade stiffened beside me. I didn't want another enemy, but if I had one, then I wanted all of the information I could get on it.

The king nodded. "An ercho is a demon spawn of the Dark One. This fae stays in the shadows and we have never been able to destroy him. The darkness has never been content to stay in the banished lands of the Otherworld, but until now we were strong enough to keep them at bay. We couldn't wipe them out completely, but we could keep them from taking over everything. Now ... if they have sided with the winter and fall courts, there is no telling what power they might have."

I didn't like where this conversation was going. I had too many wars to worry about. The king stepped closer to me and lowered his voice. "Fix the mecca, give us back our health and life, and when the time comes we will fight to the death with you against the demons."

Dammit. There went my hope that after fixing the mecca I could just live happily ever after.

We need this alliance, Kade told me.

I agree, I replied.

I reached out my hand to the king and met his steely gaze. "We will fix the mecca, and should the war come, we will help you cull the demons."

The prince looked pleased, as did his father, who extended his hand to grasp mine. "I pledge my greatest warriors and magic born on the day that the demons leave their dark cave and come for you."

We shook on it, and I prayed like hell it never came to that.

Caspien pointed to my ears. "I knew from the first day we met that you were connected to the Winter Court. You smelled like one of the highborn, but I couldn't figure out how it was possible."

I nodded. "Yes, I am half Winter Court fae, but I claim nothing from them. We make our own destinies; we're not born into them."

The king smiled. "I know that to be true."

I curtsied again. "It has been a true pleasure to speak with you. We are very thankful for all of your help. Especially for the healing of my friend. I must return home now and fix the mecca. There is no more time to waste."

Kade shook the king's hand and then we were walking briskly back to where my friends awaited. As much as my mind wanted to mull through all of this demon and ercho business, I had more pressing matters right now. So I stuffed it deep down where I put everything else that was too big or horrible to deal with, and decided I'd pull it back up when I needed to.

As we neared, the summer soldiers took to one knee and bowed their respect toward Kade and me. At the same time, the two magic born stepped into view. They were carrying a large piece of reflective glass, like a mirror but more opaque. It was placed against a tree, and then both spent many moments hovering their hands across it.

As the time passed, their words grew softer, and their bodies hunched forward. Their haggard expressions worried me as they slowly brought a swirling portal to life across the reflective surface. I swallowed my gasp when they both slumped forward, clearly unconscious.

"Will they be okay?" I asked Caspien, who stood close by.

The prince nodded. "They will sleep for a few days, but otherwise will be fine. Opening portals between our two worlds is extremely difficult."

The portal now filled the entire piece of glass, at least six feet wide and ten feet tall, flames roaring in front of it. I peered through and my heart lifted as I recognized the inside of Baladar's loft.

"I gave them a little direction," Violet whispered close to my side. "I didn't fancy having to take a dip in the lake today."

I'd bet that they hadn't even know they were getting a little help from Violet. Seemed she had learned a few things in her time in the Otherworld.

Giving all of the fae around me one last nod, I turned to my friends. "Let's go home."

Despite the darkness of the king's message, I could only be grateful that we were all returning in one piece. Technically, our journey into the fae world had ended in happiness. Violet was alive. Everything I had gone through was worth it. I would go to the ends of the Earth and far beyond for my best friend.

She caught my eye and a wonky grin crossed her face. "Let's go have ourselves snake burgers for dinner, eh?"

My smile grew wider. "You just read my mind."

**

The moment I stepped through to Earth, the force of the mecca almost slammed me to my knees. It was so strong over here, and after being in the Otherworld, with their weakness, I almost couldn't handle the overflow. My fae energy swirled as it smashed into the mecca side of my power. My hands formed tight fists at my sides as I gritted my teeth and tried not to lose it. The shifter gods only knew what havoc I might cause if I lost it now. With a final surge of effort, I managed to lock some of the power down, long enough for the rest of it to settle in my core.

Straightening I recognized the room we had stepped into, it was the sitting area where Baladar had served us tea. This time, though, there was nothing magical about the area. It was now a large, sterile-looking parlor holding a few dusty pieces of furniture, and one ragged, gray, worn out magic born sitting in the lotus position, eyes closed, hands steady across his knees.

I rushed forward, toward him. "Baladar!"

Calista let out a squeak, distracting me as she jumped to her feet. I hadn't noticed her at first, my attention firmly locked on the magic born, but now I took in her pale features, which showcased both shock and relief as she took a few hurried steps toward me, wrapping me up in one of her hugs.

I hugged her back hard, trying not to cry as her familiar warmth and love washed over me. She was the closest thing I had to a mother, and after meeting my father and grandmother, I was more grateful than ever for her.

"What happened?" she choked out as she pulled back, scanning across me. "We've been trying to reach you. I thought you were dead."

Her voice got all screechy and she was shaking a little, her eyes locking onto my face. She reached up, her fingers drifting over my pointy ears, but she didn't freak out or demand to know what happened. She just smiled. I could feel her emotions. She was simply grateful I had returned alive.

I pulled her back to me, hugging her as tightly as I could. "I'm sorry, I was taken captive by the winter queen and we only just escaped. I've returned as soon as I could."

I heard her breath catch when I spoke of the winter queen, and she burrowed herself even tighter into me. "Thank the gods you're okay."

I pulled back and turned my concern toward Baladar. He had not moved even though there were now half a dozen or more shifters in his home. He remained in that meditative position. "What happened to him? Is this Selene's doing?" I stepped closer, and flinched as I brushed against a wall of energy surrounding him.

Calista hurried back to her former lover's side, seemingly unbothered by the energy. "It's sort of to do with Selene. Her war, anyway. Baladar has been holding time."

Say what now? Kian let out a surprised sound, but I couldn't focus on him. I needed answers. "What does that mean, Cal?"

She had her creased brow and her huge eyes focused on Baladar again. "It means that normally weeks would have passed here during the days you were in the Otherworld. Which meant you would miss the war. So we decided to try and slow things down. This spell is very powerful, so only a few days have passed since you left for the Otherworld – almost equal time actually. Baladar has used all of his strength to hold time ... or more accurately slow it down. It's lucky you arrived back when you did. He is almost out of energy, and even with all our delaying, Selene will be launching her first strike tomorrow."

It looked to me like he had almost killed himself in the process on trying to stop this war.

Violet stepped closer, her expression somber. "Time magic is not something any magic born should attempt." Darkness flickered in the depths of her icy eyes, and I just knew my normally jovial friend had been broken in the land of the fae. I wondered if she would ever be the same again.

Baladar's eyes flicked open then, and half the room took a step back. I just barely stopped myself. His irises were no longer pale blue with lightning through them, nope. Now his entire eye was pure white.

"I'm very old and wise," he said to Violet, his voice no more than a croak. "I influenced only what I needed to, and any consequences of this time slip which may arise will hopefully be worth it if it saves the shifter races."

Calista placed a hand on his arm and he smiled. "I would do anything to save my people," he said with conviction.

He turned and looked directly at me. It was not an expression I'd seen from him before. It was like he was looking just beyond, or through me.

"Are you blind now?" I asked hesitantly. *Please say no. Please say no.* I would never ask for this sacrifice for him.

My heart cracked when he nodded. "It would seem so."

"We don't know if it's temporary or permanent," Calista broke in. "He will need a long time to recover his energy, and I pray his sight returns with it."

She was trying to be positive, but it was clear she didn't truly believe what she had said. I knew from the look on her face.

Baladar stood. "I still have *the sight*, and that's the only thing I care to see. Arianna, you must go now and prepare for war. I've seen many outcomes, always changing, but the one that benefits you the most is when you act less like the cold Red Queen and more like a mother protecting her children. Good luck."

A loud crack pierced the room, and two butterflies began to flit about Baladar's head. "Time is back to moving at normal speed now. Go."

Holy crap. No pressure. *A mother protecting her children?* That was nice and vague. Calista hurried forward to assist Baladar, settling him into a nearby chair, and with one last lingering look, left his side to approach me. "There's a vortex back to Staten Island that is ready to go. We should get going so we can start planning our next move."

She looked toward Baladar, her eyes creasing downwards as she blinked a few times. I shook my head, putting an arm on her shoulder. "Calista, you're temporarily removed from duty."

Her entire face crumbled as emotion overtook her. She stared up at me, unblinking. Finally she said, "What … why?"

I let my eyes rest on Baladar, looking like half the shifter he had been when we last saw him. "Take care of him for me. That's an order," I said with as much conviction as I could. "He has done more than anyone to help, and prevent this war. Now he needs you."

She gave me a small smile. "Are you sure? There could still be a war … with Selene … who is probably one of the evilest shifters I have ever met. Baladar and I both understand the sacrifice. We made our peace with it."

She was trying to convince me, but I knew her strong sense of duty would never let her heart choose what it wanted. I was going to make sure she got her choice for once.

I pulled her in for another hug. "Just follow your heart," I whispered in her ear. "You both deserve a chance at happiness." When I pulled back, she looked sad but also strong, like a weight had been lifted from her shoulders and she was ready to take on the world.

Kade stepped into my side. "You can email Gerald on our private server," he said. "Any ideas you have will be brought to the war room."

His reassurance that she would still be involved added a layer of acceptance and gratitude to her expression. She took one last look between the king and me, then gave us both a nod before she stepped back to put a hand on Baladar's shoulder.

I turned to the group, all of them waiting in silence. "Let's go get my crown back."

My words were laced with energy, with conviction, and with slices of anger. Now that I was back on Earth, away from the immediate worry of Violet's death, I let some of my anger toward Selene filter out. Today was her last day as queen of the wolf shifters.

Violet smiled, the first real one since we'd stepped back to Earth, and in that smile I saw death. I was right there with her. It had been Selene and Sabina's magic blanket that had allowed the fae to slip through and attack that night of the mid-summer festival. The very night Violet was stolen away. We still didn't know if they were working with the winter queen and this new mysterious dark power. If I had learned anything from my so-called father, it was that the fae had been trying to find a powerful ally on

Earth for many years. Maybe they had finally found one.

Calista gave us directions to the tree that hid the bears' vortex disc, and we made our way into Baladar's garden. The mecca energy was strong in this section. I could feel the vortex.

Blaine stepped forward. "Your Majesties, let me go first in case it's a trap."

He unsheathed his fae sword, which had somehow survived the trip across. Mine had been stripped from me when I was taken captive, and I wished it was still here. Kade gave him a single nod, and I did the same, even though my insides were frozen. For the first time he had addressed us both as his rulers, and alongside that shock was hope that maybe the bears and wolves could rule side by side.

"Thank you," I said. "And be safe."

Blaine stepped onto the disc, vanishing in an instant. Victor and Monica followed right after.

Kade turned to his brother then, who was waiting patiently with his family. "I'll go through first, to make sure it's all secure. I'll leave Nix here with you so I can send word if it's safe. She'll shriek twice to alert you. Then you can come across." He turned to his magic born. "Nikoli, can you make sure they're safe during the journey across?"

Nikoli, who was standing very close to Violet –
I'd noticed that he hadn't been far from her since
the moment I saw them all again in the Winter
Court – gave his king a nod.

"I will protect them with my life."

"I'll help him," Violet added, her tone hard to
read.

I wanted to protest. I didn't want her out of
my sight, but I knew she would never accept me
overprotecting her. I had to let go and trust in
her ability to keep herself safe. Baladar's home
was secure, and this vortex should only lead to
Staten Island, so I really had very little to worry
about … which helped in no way at all.

Nix took off from Kade's shoulder, hovering
just above Kian and his family's heads. Kade and
I stepped on the disc – Finn remained close to
my side. I took a deep breath. This was the first
time I would travel in the vortex since finding
out about my mother … about the Red Queen. It
had been her voice in the vortex this entire time,
and I wondered if she would try to contact me.
Part of me was hoping she would, so I could hear
her voice again, could ask her the million and
five questions I had. Another part of me knew
there was no time right now to deal with it.
Unless she had some information or a weapon
which could help in this war, a reunion would
have to wait.

As Kade took my hand, I felt that familiar pull of mecca and let it take me, sucking me through the magical lines. I was tense the entire time, waiting to hear that chiming voice ... but for once there was nothing.

In a blink, we were at the bench seat on Staten Island. Finn took off immediately, briefly saying: *Will scout for trouble. Keep an eye on the vortex until everyone else is through.*

Thanks, buddy.

I focused back on Kade, who had tilted his head down, his eyes asking me all the questions. I shook my head as we both stepped off the disc to get out of the way of the others coming through. "I didn't hear her. There was nothing at all."

His arms went around me then, lifting me up into his body as he gave one of those big bear hugs, a hug I was quickly becoming addicted to, like his strength alone was enough to keep me together. I could only hope I offered him the same comfort.

"We'll figure it out. Once we return the mecca to the Otherworld, we can focus on the Red Queen. On how she is using the vortex to speak with you."

Rising up on my toes to stretch as tall as I could – and still only reaching his chin – I smashed my lips against Kade's. He was in my corner no matter what the world threw at me. A true partner in every single sense. Was there anything sexier than someone who completely and totally had your back?

Hell no there wasn't.

Our kiss was just getting heated, Kade's hands somehow finding their way under my fur coat to cup my butt and lift me closer to him, when the roar of engines broke through our haze of emotion. I was breathing hard when I pulled away. Kade reluctantly lowered me to the ground, although he kept an arm around me. As we turned toward the approaching vehicles, Blaine, Monica, and Victor walked into view, stopping close by us. I'd actually forgotten that they were already here. No doubt they had been giving us some privacy, but as the two SUVs closed in on us, pulling up by the curb, they were back on guard duty.

Gerald, Annette – Kade's mother – and Jen my dominant who had stayed behind to be on the bear council, were all there with excitement on their faces.

Annette reached us first and she pulled me in for a hug. I was surrounded by warmth and energy and it was very clear where Kade had learned to hug so thoroughly.

"Thank the gods! You've returned safe and sound." She pulled back when she saw my ears and blinked a few times, reaching out to graze her fingertips across them. The slightest of frowns crossed her lovely face. "Well, that's interesting."

Interesting wasn't even close to covering it. "Yes, a lot happened in the Otherworld. It's a long story though. There will be time later to go over everything. First though ... we have some news for you."

Kade took over then, stepping closer so his mother could wrap her arms tightly around him. I could just hear his low voice as he said, "Kian's alive, Ma. He was trapped in the fae lands."

The words had barely left his mouth when the vortex started making a popping noise behind us. Before I could even turn, Kade's mother let out a cry, one filled with so much emotion I had tears pricking my eyes. Then she was running, pushing through all of us and leaping onto Kian. Seeing a mother reunited with a child, weeping in happiness, it brought a happy ache to my heart. Not just mine either, by the looks of the leaky eyes and cleared throats going on around us. Even Gerald, the big toughie, had shiny eyes.

Violet, standing close to my side, even reached out and gave my hand a brief graze. Neither of us looked at the other, but I could feel her torn emotions, her joy and sorrow. Her time in the Otherworld was still controlling her, but she would take this one moment to feel a sliver of happiness. Might as well take them where we could. We both knew there would be many dark days ahead of us.

Finn, who was back from scouting, pressed into my legs. I dropped my hands down into his thick fur. After that very emotional reunion, Annette led us to the cars and we split into two groups. I got into the first vehicle with Kade, Violet, Blaine, Monica, Finn, and Gerald, who was driving. Nix and Kian's familiar, whose name I learned was Jota, took to the air. They would follow us in their preferred mode of transport: flight.

Leaning forward, I said to Gerald, "How did you know to meet us here?"

Kade's war councilman chuckled as he started the powerful car and pulled away. "Calista emailed me a few minutes ago. Annette had us all out the door in about eight seconds. We've been so worried. The shifter world needs its leaders." He cleared his throat a little. "We need our friends."

It was totally a hugging moment, but Gerald was driving, so I settled for a hand on his shoulder.

"How's Winnie?" I missed my little sister dearly and wanted to make sure Selene couldn't get to her. One of the things on my to-do list was to ensure she was not touched by this war. I would protect her innocence.

Gerald turned down Kade's street, heading toward the gates to his huge estate. "Winnie is safe on the Island, running the bear house like it's her own. She has staff at her fingertips and she's with some of the other bear children. Both parties have agreed to the Island being neutral ground. The pregnant women and children have all been moved there."

A surge of relief pretty much knocked me back into my seat. Selene might have a sliver of decency after all. Of course, a sliver wasn't enough to make up for all the damage she had caused, and I would not soften my stance on her one bit. The gates to Kade's estate opened and the car pulled slowly in. As we got closer to the house, we saw the grounds were littered with a bunch of tents and RVs. A low gasp slipped out as I again leaned forward in my seat, trying to see everything.

Wolf shifters!

There were wolf shifters milling around the camp.

"Are they prisoners?" I murmured. They didn't look like prisoners, but it was the most logical thing I could think of in times of war.

The car parked and Gerald turned back to look at me. His normally hard eyes seemed softer. "No, Queen Arianna. They're defectors. Said they will only fight for you. There are more too. Many have remained in the boroughs, but have pledged to fight for the resistance. You're not alone."

A sob rose in my throat but I pushed it down. Now was the time for strength, but still ... my people were here. They'd risked their lives and went against all of their traditions to come to bear territory. Just to be by my side in the dark days ahead. Gerald reached over and patted my hand. "We get more and more every day. They're camping on the beach, in our rental homes. We actually can't house them all. There are hundreds."

I let out a steady breath, still working hard to keep the tears at bay. I would exit this car and be the queen they expected, not a blubbering mess. Kade's hand came up to wrap around my shoulder, his strong fingers gently rubbing my tense muscles.

"Let's do this," he said.

Sucking in a deep breath, I nodded a few times, calming and centering myself. I could do this. I was the queen they wanted, and I would take Selene out so I could unite my people again and fight against the real threat. The winter fae.

My car door opened and I stepped out. I was covered in dirt and dried blood. I had pointy ears and foreign features, but when my people saw me they fell to their knees, bowing in respect.

I slowly walked past each and every one of them, shaking the men's hands and hugging the women. I looked each one in the eye and thanked them for supporting me. I promised them I would fix this and get our home back.

An alpha wolf stepped forward then, bringing with her a strong aura of mecca power. I recognized her immediately: Bianca, the alpha of Boston. The one with more than a little influence in the shifter world. She gave me a low head nod, and then stepped closer. "I am very pleased to see you returned safely, and with our stolen magic born no less. You have proven to be the very leader I anticipated and hoped for, one who could do great things for our packs."

I returned her nod, mine subtler. "Thank you, I appreciate your support. I'm going to do everything in my power to prevent this war. I will remove Selene from power and I will take back my crown."

I was channeling Calista with my positive affirmations for the day.

Bianca's large eyes were very dark, almost reflective. She turned to gaze at the many wolves standing close by, listening to our words. "A queen is only as strong as her people, without support any leader is weakened. Selene is weak right now. Do us proud, and we will carry you through the toughest of battles."

She reached out her hand, adorned in many glittering jewels, and I didn't hesitate to clasp my own to it. With a shake I let my happiness spill across my face in a broad smile. "I will do you proud. Now if you'll excuse me, I have a battle to prepare for."

A huge cheer went up, and Bianca seemed pleased as she stepped back, allowing me and the others to pass through.

Once we were through the crowds, making our way to the mansion, I noticed that Kian's expression was quite emotional, his eyes looking lost as he stared up at the house. The look on his face was a mixture of sadness and unbridled joy.

Annette, who had not moved very far from her returned son's side, wrapped her arms around him and said something quietly that I couldn't hear. Whatever it was, Kian seemed happier as he pressed a kiss to his mother's cheek. Kade and I were the first up onto the porch, everyone else following close by. I felt a sense of home wash over me, I loved this estate so much.

Gerald brought me back to reality by saying, "We have readied the war room."

Just like that, expressions sobered, shoulders straightened, and we were in warrior mode. It was time to plan Selene's demise and fix the mecca before it tore both of our worlds apart.

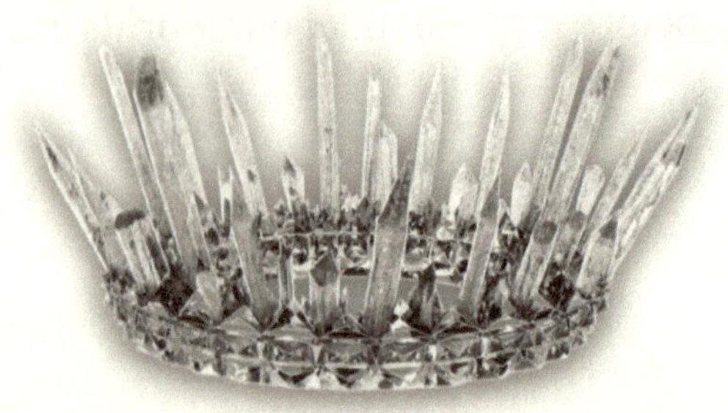

Chapter Thirteen

Why do the best plans always end with a murder?

"NO! I REFUSE to let my people be slaughtered." I stood in the war room with Kade, Gerald, Violet, Annette, Nikoli, and Kian. We were surrounding the round table with the boroughs map. Nix and Jota were on the men's shoulders; Finn was standing tall at my side, offering his support as I pressed my point further. "We want minimal casualties. This isn't a real war. My people are being used as pawns by Selene and the council."

Violet had been quiet during most of the arguing and discussion. I recognized her expression, the one she used when she was deep in thought, calculating something huge. So far tons of ideas had been thrown around, but they all involved brute force and the possibility of massive casualties on both sides. I had to worry about my own people and Kade's.

It was stupid and frustrating trying to deal with this fake war. If I were still queen, none of this would be happening. Meanwhile, we were not even remotely prepared to face the fae, who would be true enemies in every sense of the word.

Violet finally stood, interrupting our arguments. "We're going about this all wrong. The only thing in Arianna's way is Selene."

"What are you saying?" Kade asked, more gruffness than usual in his voice. It was near midnight and the terms of war were that by 5 A.M tomorrow morning all bets were off. Word was that Selene had her army camped out at the vortexes, and that she was going to openly attack at first light. Kade's people were ready on their side of the magical discs, but I wanted a solution that didn't result in mass casualties.

Violet shrugged. "This war doesn't even need to happen. What needs to happen is Selene gets gutted with a dull knife."

I was torn between smiling and worrying. Violet had always been brutal and reckless in her own way, but it felt like she was ten times worse now. I feared she would do something to get herself killed because she was trying to assuage the pain inside of her.

"What are you saying? Assassination? Just sneak in there before the war even starts and kill Selene?"

Violet nodded, her thin arms crossed over her chest. Baladar had said not to be like the Red Queen, be more like a mother protecting her children. The Red Queen would go for the all-out war, killing those who stood against her, making sure no one dared to ever stand against her again. But maybe Violet was right. I didn't want to punish my people for siding with Selene or being too scared to speak up. I really just wanted that crazy bitch out of power so I could protect my people from the real threat, the winter fae.

"Assassination..." I let the word roll off my tongue. Kill Selene and Sabina, fire the council, and let the people decide. I could rule them again or they could choose to call another Summit. Let the new heir lead them and I would step down. Maybe it was time the wolves did something a little different. Maybe the leader should be the one chosen by the people, not by an ancient law that didn't even make sense.

I stood straighter, taking in the full map of the boroughs before me. "Violet is right ... I think we should take Selene out before the war begins." I stabbed my finger down on the Manhattan vortex. It was time for all of my mecca chess training and battle strategy. "She'll most likely be here somewhere, but it's going to be very hard to find her. The Red Queen used to have a battle strategy of having Sabina spell a few decoys to look like her, so we can assume Selene would do the same. It's something I would do as well. I need to know which is the real one – I'll only have one chance. If she knows I'm coming, she'll go into hiding. So we need a plan. It has to be the best plan we have ever created, and we have five hours to do it all!"

I expected them to freeze or freak out and tell me it couldn't be done, but no one did that. Instead they stepped up, they acted like leaders, and we worked out how to take the wolf queen down.

Kian, who had been looking quite thoughtful, finally said: "You need to figure out how to tap into your Tuatha side. They have powers above and beyond the shifters. And you are something I have never seen before."

Thanks, buddy.

"You have a dual heritage," Kade said. "Shifters might have been born of human and fae, but you're the first shifter to be born of fae and shifter. And your mother and father are both heirs. This gives you an unprecedented tie to the mecca. You're ten times more powerful than Selene. We just need to work out how to utilize this."

"What sort of things can the winter queen do?" I was looking at Kian. He was our fae expert now. "Besides the ice breath."

He took a second to think. "She can freeze someone's power. She can force mecca back into an individual and kill them that way. She can control the will of those weaker. She can influence minds. She can open portals anywhere there is a mecca stone and step through—"

I threw a hand up, interrupting him mid-flow. "She can open a portal to a mecca stone? Like a vortex?"

Kian nodded. "Yes, she is one of the only fae leaders who can do this ... it was inherited by her son."

"Which explains how I can do it too. I thought it was a glitch that the portal opened into the fae lands for us, but clearly not."

Kade said, "If you manage to open a vortex into that mecca stone room, then what will you do?"

"I will send the mecca back to the fae. Selene will feel the loss of power. She'll know it's me, then she will come for me." I turned to Violet. "I might need your help seeing and guiding the power."

Violet nodded. "It's not a full moon, so I might not be able to completely share my power with you, but I'll do what I can."

It would have to be good enough. I would figure it out somehow.

Kade clenched his fists on the side of the table. "How do you know Selene won't bring her entire army?"

My eyes had been locked on the map, on my territories. I looked up to answer him. "I don't think she will. Selene knows I'm the one weakness in her plans. She knows the people are not fully on her side. This is personal for her. She's going to try and take me out alone. Prove she is stronger. Her ego will get the best of her."

Violet backed me up. "Selene and Arianna have been locked in a power struggle for many years, one which Ari almost always beats her at. Taking the crown was the first time Selene ever came out on top. She'll do everything in her power to make sure she not only keeps the crown, but is the hero to the people. She'll attempt to kill Arianna herself, I'm sure of it."

"I will be there too," Kade said. "You, me, and Violet. All of us will be needed to shift the power back to the Otherworld."

And me, Finn said in my mind, his voice firm.

I looked down at him, shaking my head and speaking out loud. "The familiars should stay behind. We need to sneak in and out, and three of us is already turning into a crowd."

How about if we wait for you at Baladar's? Then we will be nearby if you need us.

That I could live with, so I gave him and the eagle a single nod. "Waiting at Baladar's is a great plan."

I definitely looked like a crazy person talking to myself, but everyone around me understood. It wasn't the first time Finn and I had carried on a conversation like that. I felt some sense of relief that a plan was set into motion. A plan which would hopefully have minimal casualties. Selene did not count. She had started all of this after all.

Please let this work. We had already lost too many shifters in this pointless bear versus wolf life we lived. It didn't even make any logical sense. We were all the same, pretty much.

Annette and Gerald moved to the door then. "We will still ready the bears," the war councilman said. "I have the rest of the council members arranging our warriors at the vortexes, in case you aren't successful. Not that I'm worried." He gave me a wink. "Good luck, sir." That was for Kade, and then they were gone.

The others followed soon after, Kade the last to leave. "I'll check in with my people and be right back. Meet you at the door," he said as he pressed his lips to my forehead, before striding from the room.

I stayed behind with Finn to study the board for a few more minutes. Violet got halfway out before doubling back to my side. I was surprised as her hand wrapped tightly around my forearm. She never usually touched me like this, with such a firm grip.

"Sabina is mine." Her voice was fierce and growly.

I took a moment to really see her. We had been running or fighting since the moment we'd found her in the Otherworld. I'd had no chance to really look at my best friend. Her suffering was written across every part of her face. Her pale eyes were dull, with dark circles beneath them. Her skin looked washed out, less of the vibrant glow than she normally wore. Even the leather outfit, so unlike her normal clothes, made her seem small and vulnerable.

She was broken, and she was worrying me. "Are you sure you're up to all this? I mean..."

You were tortured almost beyond repair, is what I left unsaid.

Violet swallowed hard, her eyes locked on a spot just behind me, like she couldn't look me in the eye any longer. Her next words were hoarse: "Being near death changes you, Ari. No longer will I cater to the whims of those who don't deserve my respect or loyalty. Sabina crossed the wrong magic born." She paused and I was relieved to find her meeting my eyes again. "Plus, I don't want to waste time anymore. I want to live life fully."

I chuckled. "And by live life fully, you mean rip Sabina's head off?"

She grinned and said, "Exactly." The sight of her smile filled me with a burst of hot, deep emotions. I could imagine it was akin to seeing your child smile for the first time, like an accomplishment.

Unable to help myself, and since she seemed to be all about the physical contact today, I pulled my dear friend in for a hug. As her scent washed over me I tried not to become too emotional. "I love you, Vi," I murmured against her shoulder. It had to be said. One, or both of us, might not live past this night, and I needed her to know how much she meant to me. "I know you're hurting right now and I want you to know that you can take as long as you need to deal with what happened in the Otherworld. It was a big deal. You need some time."

I could feel her chest shaking under me, but her voice was clear as she said, "Not as much as I love you, sister."

When we pulled apart, we were both misty-eyed. Swallowing down the massive lump in my throat, I forced a smile. "I'd better toughen up if I'm about to take on Selene. No weeping."

Violet returned my smile. "The weeping is what makes you stronger than Selene, Ari."

Then she patted my shoulder and left the room. As I turned back to the board, I stopped and gave myself five minutes to really think about everything that had happened recently, everything I had learned, especially about myself. It was shocking, but at the same time made sense to me. I mean, I would never have guessed my father was a full-blown fae prince, and an asshole – well, actually, that part I could have easily guessed. And as much as I had loved my pseudo-mother, she had always raised me at arm's reach, which made a lot more sense now that I knew I wasn't biologically hers. Of course the Red Queen had acted the same way, so maybe that was just the sisters' way.

Finn remained silently at my side, just being there, like he always had. *I never needed them. I had you,* I said to him, his love warming my heart.

A knock at the war room door drew my attention. It was Annette, and she was carrying a portable landline handset.

"A certain five year old refuses to sleep until she talks to you. She overheard the news that you were back."

A huge grin broke out across my face as I grabbed the phone and pressed it to my ear.

"Winnie, I missed you so much, baby girl! Are you okay?"

"Sissy! I missed you too." Her sweet cherubic voice cut right into my heart. I had to take down Selene, I refused to miss seeing my beautiful sister again. I wanted to be there when she grew up.

"Did you get Auntie Violet back?" she asked, the last part of her words cut off by a huge yawn.

"I did, Win. She's safe and sound. I'll get her to call you later. Now I think it's bedtime for you, little one. I will come and get you very soon. There are just a few things I need to fix in Manhattan first."

God, please don't let this be the last time I heard this sweet voice.

"Okay, Ari. Love you." She was nearly asleep. I could tell by the sluggishness in her voice.

"Love you too, bunny. Night, night." I hung up the phone, holding the receiver tightly. I could feel the plastic cracking under the pressure, so I eased up, staring down at the table, willing myself not to lose it. A cleared throat startled me, and I realized Annette was still standing in the doorway. I'd totally forgotten she was there. She crossed over to me now and I extended my hand with the phone in it, guessing that was what she wanted. She did take it, but only to set it aside on the table.

She stepped closer, towering over me, and tipped my chin up to meet her eyes. "Winnie is an amazing little girl. You're doing a great job, especially with all your other responsibilities."

I shook my head. "She gets pushed aside for duty all the time, just as I was growing up. I know she has luxury and staff, but nothing replaces family."

Annette tilted her head to the side, observing me with her wise eyes. "I didn't know who my parents were, just the same as you."

Her blunt confession caught me off guard. "You didn't?" I never knew that about her.

She shook her head. "I was discarded and left on the doorstep of a den in Staten Island. The rumors were that I was the result of an affair between a single woman and a married man. Dropped off to the closest bear community."

"That must have been hard, not knowing where you came from." It was hitting deep in my soul right now because it was hard for me too.

She shrugged. "Not really. What I wanted to tell you is that you don't need to know where you came from to know where you're going. You don't need to be anything like the winter prince or the Red Queen. Those are just genetics. The woman who just spoke to her five year old sister is *nothing* like the Red Queen."

Her reassurance touched me. I had been having this growing fear that I was somehow innately evil because of my parentage, but what she said eased some of my worry. I wasn't like them and I wouldn't be. I would forge my own destiny.

I straightened, a genuine smiling tilting up my lips. "Thank you," I said. "You have no idea how much I needed to hear that. The reality is, Calista is the reason we turned out so well. She's been a true mother to me and Winnie. She's the mother of my heart."

Annette smiled as she smoothed my hair, which was loose and unruly. "Give Selene hell, child. Then come home and celebrate. I'm throwing a party for Kian and Violet's safe return, to celebrate my grandbaby and daughter-in-law who I am blessed enough to know now. I want to add a newly-crowned queen to that agenda."

I smiled. I had certainly lucked out having a future mother-in-law that was so cool. "Oh I plan to give her a lot more than hell."

Selene had stripped me of my crown, my dignity, my family. I was going to exterminate her.

Annette and Finn were by my side as I left the room, though they both gave me some privacy to say goodbye to my dominants, who were waiting for me. They were silent, and I could tell from their faces that they had been filled in on the plan.

Blaine was right in my face, channeling the pushy little kid he had been in our youth. "We should be with you, Ari!"

Leaning forward, I wrapped my arms around him. It was a night for hugs, for goodbyes. "It's too dangerous. This is a stealth mission, which means we need minimal people."

Blaine returned my hug so hard my ribs creaked in protest, but I didn't say anything. I would take this, I would take whatever I had to for my family. "I'll come back to you, I promise." I said this to each of them as Monica, Jen, and Victor all got their chance for a hug.

Then it was time to get out of here. Time to get my crown back.

**

Kade, Violet, and I stood at the vortex that would take us to Baladar's loft. Once we were back in Manhattan, we would sneak into the royal estate and send the mecca back. It should be even easier than last time, because all of the army was out of the estate, at the vortexes, readying to take on the bears. Finn and Nix, who were supposed to head straight to Baladar's, had informed us that they would go through first and scout.

They were already out in the alleys of Manhattan. As per usual, they had ignored my request, but I couldn't be too mad, as now we had some up-to-date intel. Finn said the city was crawling with guards, but that from what they overheard, Selene wasn't in the borough center. She'd left to check on her people manning the waterway between Manhattan and Staten Island.

"Lucky Baladar was able to change the times this vortex was functional," I said, sitting on the bench with Kade and Violet. "Wednesday would have been a little late."

It was Saturday, mid-August. By Wednesday many shifters would be dead. Our battles were fast and lethal.

Kade's strong hand slipped into mine, more of a comfort than the weight of the sword at my hip. I no longer had my fae blade, that had been lost when the winter queen took me in the Otherworld. This blade was more than enough to take out Selene though.

We connected to Manhattan and Staten Island disappeared from around us, the familiar energy sucking us through to Baladar's loft. Last time we were here, the environment had been dim and muted, the flowers dull, a clear sign of Baladar's poor health and loss of power. Everything now looked just a little more vibrant, and I hoped that meant my friend was on the mend. We stepped out from under the tree and crossed the large garden, heading for a door on the far wall.

Footsteps to my left had me turning with my sword raised. Upon seeing Calista, I lowered the weapon. "Cal, you scared me."

She gave me a smile. "I knew you would choose to sneak in and take out Selene before letting any of your people get hurt."

"Am I that easy to read?" I said with a chuckle.

She shook her head, soft strands of brown hair falling in front of her eyes. "No, but I raised you right, so I know how you think."

My throat tightened. The Red Queen might have been my biological mother, but I meant what I'd said to Annette. Calista was the mother of my heart. She was the mother I chose.

I ate up the gap between us. She reached out and grasped my hand. "I'm going to fix this," I whispered.

Calista nodded, a fierce determination lining her ageless face. "I never doubted you for a second. You are kind and strong, two things Selene knows nothing about." Her voice got very serious. "Just remember, Selene's weakness is her overconfidence. She is high on power and you can use that to your advantage. Her ego will be her downfall."

I was counting on that. Her support gave me a boost of adrenalin; she had just confirmed the information we had built our entire plan on. I felt much better about it now. Calista was brilliant at mecca chess; I based many of my own strategic plays on hers. "Learn your enemy" was rule number one, and luckily, after many years of clashes, I knew everything about Selene and that slimy snake.

"Say it," Calista said, and I chuckled. Still, it felt right to have this moment.

"I will kill Selene! I will take back the crown! I will win!" The fierceness in my voice assured me I was more than ready to achieve these goals. Achieve them or die trying.

As Kade always said, an honorable death was worth much. But I preferred to live for many more years. I had plenty of honor to last me the distance. Calista nodded, looking every bit the proud mother. Leaning over, I kissed her on the cheek, and then it was time to leave. Turning on my heel, I followed Kade and Violet out of the door and into a fight for my life.

For my crown. For my people.

Chapter Fourteen

Mother dearest.

FINN HADN'T BEEN kidding when he said the streets of Manhattan were filled with guards. They were everywhere. Of course, Selene had them decked out in bright purple shirts, the color of her heir line, which made it fairly easy to spot and avoid them. Finn and Nix were giving us feedback as they cruised through the streets. Neither of them would return to Baladar's loft, but they were at least staying out of sight, even though both of them were pretty unhappy about not being able to join us.

At about 3 A.M most of the patrols halted and the guards started marching their way through Manhattan.

Selene is calling them to the vortex, Kade said. We were hiding out in a small alley, letting the masses stream past us.

I nodded once at him, but remained vigilant. The moment the street was clear, we were going to have to haul butt to make it in time. 5 A.M was the deadline.

Finn tried again to guilt me into letting him closer. *Ari, we're stronger together.*

I know. Once all the guards are gone, come find me at the royal estate. We'll be in the mecca stone room.

He was satisfied, and I fought against the instinct to order him back to bear territory, far away from the danger. But if I had learned anything from my time with the winter fae, it was that I couldn't do it all alone, that Finn and I were essentially the same soul. If I died, so would he. I just wasn't keen on it being the other way around. I'd still live if he died, but I wouldn't want to.

"We should be able to go in ninety seconds," Violet said from behind me. She was letting Kade and I have the lookout.

I swiveled to see her better, the dim light reflecting off her pale beauty. "Ninety seconds?" That was oddly specific, even for her.

She gave me a wink, and it almost felt like the old Violet was back. For a moment.

"I know things. Sometimes the universe is my friend." Her cryptic reply didn't bother me. I accepted her secrets.

The seconds ticked by, and sure enough, almost exactly a minute and half later, the streets were empty. The quiet seemed extra eerie after all the noise that had just been echoing around. Kade took point, ducking out first. I followed close behind, and I could feel Violet's energy right there with me. We stuck to the shadows. I sensed Nix right above us, which was reassuring. She was pretty great at spotting problems before they arose.

Kade took us a roundabout route, which was frustrating because time was running out. Selene wasn't supposed to attack for another two hours, but I didn't trust her to keep true to that. My nails were pretty much chewed to the bone now, nerves harassing me with the force of a small storm.

As we crossed the street to find ourselves near the back entrance of the royal garden, I had to smile. "We really need to try something new for our next date." I winked at Kade.

He brushed his thumb down my cheek. "What, sneaking into an abandoned palace on the brink of war isn't romantic enough?"

Suddenly a guard jumped out in front of us and Kade drew his sword. But before either of us could act, Violet threw a spell in the guard's face and he collapsed.

Violet grinned. "That felt great! I really missed doing magic."

I sensed this freedom was cathartic for her, so I would encourage as much as I could. "Go for it, my friend. You can use magic to take Selene's people down until you've got nothing left."

"I will be," she said, as she moved forward.

Kade and I followed, stepping over the fallen guard, entering the garden. It was eerily quiet and I had the random thought that if I did survive tonight and take my crown back, where would Kade and I live? Would we have to build a house that crossed both boroughs? Or would the territories disappear altogether? Shaking my head, I discarded those thoughts. They were for another time.

We made our way to the elevator close to the back patio. Violet had sent forth some magical mojo, so it was already lit up and waiting for us, and we ran inside without pause. A streak of white ducked in at the last minute and I lunged forward to hold the doors open until Finn was fully inside. I grinned at my familiar, letting my free hand sink into his soft fur.

You're perfect with timing, you know that?

He just nuzzled my leg as the doors closed and the elevator ascended to the floor where the mecca crystal was awaiting us.

"So what's the plan? I mean ... I open a portal and then we just push mecca through it?" It was almost early morning now and I was tired. It had been a long few days in the Otherworld, and we really hadn't had the time to plan this part very well. Now that we were this close, that felt like a pretty big oversight.

Violet, who was standing stiffly near the doors, nodded a few times as if thinking it through in her head. Finally, she said, "I think we just have to go with the energy. Once you have the sight, hopefully a path becomes clear to you. Besides, the mecca is living. It will help us if this is the right thing." Her pause was brief but heavy. "The only thing to keep in mind is that whatever changed with the mecca happened when the queen died. I've had no chance to check it for any spells that may be tied to it, and I won't have time tonight. Basically, we'll just have to figure it out as we go."

Great. We were going to wing it.

Kade looked his normal calm and confident self when he said, "Nix is patrolling the skies. She'll tell us if it looks like Selene is moving early."

His confidence inspired some of my own, so when the elevator dinged I was ready, weapon held aloft. As the doors slid across, there was a tall female guard on the other side. She was relaxed, her gaze focused downwards. As she lifted her head to step inside, she saw us and her eyes widened as she stumbled back a few steps. Violet lifted her hands and I could feel the mecca energy building, but just before she released it, the guard fell to one knee.

"Your Majesty!" She bowed her head.

Violet let the magic fizzle from her hands, dissipating the spell before it could do any damage.

Stepping out of the elevator, I recognized the guard's smoky gray eyes and long blond hair, currently tied up in a top-knot. She was a friend of Monica's ... Carrie from the yellow line.

No time for anything else, I got right to the point. "Are you loyal to Selene?"

Carrie quickly shook her head, before standing. "No, Your Majesty. I tried to defect to bear territory, but she's kept us all trapped here, under the watchful eye of Sabina."

Violet growled next to me. "We're going to fix things tonight. Can we count on you to help?"

The young guard straightened and nodded, falling in behind us as we hurried along the long corridor. The closer we got to the room, the more the mecca pounded against my energy. It had my new fae side stirring to life, like a wilted plant that had been craving water and suddenly got a huge burst. It swelled within me, and I wondered if my skin looked flushed, because I was feeling very warm.

When we reached the end of the hall, I turned to Carrie. "Can you please wait here? Do whatever you can to delay anybody from entering. Tell them it's Selene's orders. Say whatever you need to give us time."

Her face paled, going a very sickly color. "Selene is ... crazy. If she hears about me helping you..."

"She won't be queen for much longer," I assured her.

Kade stepped in. "You also have the protection of me and my people. We would never leave you behind."

Carrie straightened, all doubt wiped from her face. "You can count on me."

With one last nod, Kade, Violet, Finn, and I made our way into the sitting room. I wasted no time pulling the book free and opening the door to the secret room that housed the mecca crystal. This was it, the moment I had been waiting for. We were going to fix the mecca and hopefully stop both worlds from being destroyed. And maybe, If we were lucky, we would end two wars tonight.

The blast of mecca energy coming off of the crystal was intense as we all trudged through the heavy magic to stand before it. Finn stayed on the edge of the room; Violet slotted in behind Kade and me. Maybe it was because I was now a fae, but I felt even more susceptible to the mecca's energy. My skin was tingling and tightening more with each step I took toward the stone.

"Okay, let's open up a portal and send some of this home," I said to Kade and Violet. The amount of mecca in this room was stifling, I could barely breathe.

Kade slipped his hand into mine. "I'll protect you from being overcome by it."

I nodded at my mate, and then felt Violet's hands on my back. "I'll help you too with whatever I can." As Violet had said earlier, there was no full moon, which meant she couldn't share her powers, but I hoped she could do something.

No matter what, I had to right this imbalance.

Without further ceremony, I placed my hands on the crystal and my teeth clamped down hard with the force of the mecca power that blasted into me. Without me having to do another thing, the portal to the fae lands opened before us. It was the same stretch of woods we had landed in when we went to get Violet.

"Okay, now, how do I send it through?" I said, my voice wavering as I fought against the power trying to pull me under.

'Arianna...' The Red Queen's whispery voice floated past me, and from the way Kade's hand stiffened in mine I knew he had heard her too.

"I'm here," I told the Red Queen, even though it felt stupid. She was dead, she couldn't hear me.

The crystal grew hot and my palms began to sweat.

"What the...?"

Everything around me went dark. I could no longer feel Kade's hand in mine. I was about to cry out, or blast out with my own energy, when the darkness lifted and I was suddenly standing on a sandy beach. Swallowing hard, I blinked rapidly, trying to figure out what had just happened. The ocean spanned out into the distance, and it was purple. In fact, there were tendrils of purple floating all around me. *Mecca!* I was standing in a world of visible mecca.

I turned slowly, needing to see everything. Low clouds of purple mecca rolled through the trees, through the sand, through me. A splash of red caught my attention, and I took a stumbling step closer. Her red silk dress, which was what had caught my attention, was blowing in the mecca breeze as she closed the distance between us.

The Red Queen. My mother.

My heart started pounding hard in my chest, the lump in my throat making it very hard to breathe. I didn't move. I couldn't move. She kept walking toward me, until finally she stood only a few feet away, looking as real as the last time I'd seen her alive.

"It's not possible," I murmured.

She smiled warmly, something she had never done in real life, then she reached out to touch my face, but before she could place her hand on my cheek, I flinched and stepped back.

"You're dead," I said, my voice robotic.

This must be some magic, some spell to trick me. Either Sabina or Isalinda, the winter queen, were trying to mess with me.

The Red Queen's hand lingered in the air for a moment, before she let it fall to her side. Her expression remained the same, but her eyes, which I was realizing now were the same shape as mine, looked misty. I couldn't stop staring at her, despite the fact I'd seen her many times before. Now that I knew the truth, it gave me an entirely new perspective. She was my mother ... but she also wasn't. You needed more than DNA and blood to be able to claim maternal rights.

She must have seen my anger, the coldness I could feel locking down my features. She didn't step closer as she said, "I am so sorry, Arianna. I wanted to tell you the truth a thousand times, to have you by my side where you belonged, but I couldn't. I ... I had no choice."

I swallowed the lump in my throat. "You always have a choice. How could you not tell me at least that my father was an evil fae? Look at the mess you've left the shifter world in."

She pursed her lips, giving me that icy, queenly stare I was used to. "I made a mistake in trusting him, but everything I did, I did for you, so that he wouldn't find you and kill you."

"How are you here? Where are we?"

I looked around again at the purple world.

"I knew Luca would betray me one day, so I had Sabina tie my soul to the mecca. I don't think she realized what she was doing. I worded my request very carefully. She would not have known that in the event of my death I would become one with the mecca. It was a way I could live on and keep watch over you."

I chewed my lip ... she was talking about soul magic, a magic as dangerous as time magic, from what Violet had told me. "I need to fix it. Your magic spell backfired, and when you died your energy caused the mecca to shift the balance, leaving the fae realm empty. I need to even them out to avoid war between the two lands. Not to mention this imbalance could destroy both worlds."

She raised one eyebrow. "It didn't backfire. That's what I intended. Let the fae get what they deserve." She crossed her arms and I growled.

"This isn't a time for grudges! Our people are suffering because of this. You need to help me fix it. If you really care about me, then help me." I would plead if I had to. The Red Queen had always been hardheaded, but she was showing me a softer side now, so maybe my emotional manipulation would work.

She looked off into the ocean, the purple waves were like jewels as they crested across the surface. I thought she was going to refuse me, but then she said, "Okay, Arianna ... I owe you that much."

Relief crashed through me. "Thank you."

She nodded, and then clasped my hand. Her touch was cold but still somehow warming. "I just want you to know that I never knew how to be a mother. I was raised by nannies and ... I never knew—" Her voice broke and tears lined her eyes. I stood there frozen. Never in a million years did I think the Red Queen was capable of crying. Especially over me. Feelings I didn't want to deal with were crashing into me, and the worst part was I could empathize with the Red Queen's position.

If it hadn't been for Calista, I wouldn't know how to give Winnie motherly love either. The wolf world was all about duty first and family second.

On a whim, I pulled her forward into a tight hug. "I forgive you."

Sometimes that was the best thing to do, for both parties involved. As if those words alone were powerful enough, something snapped and I was slammed back to my feet, Kade yelling beside me.

"Where were you?" he growled.

I couldn't answer, I was too busy gasping as I realized I could still see the mecca, floating in purple clouds all around. It was especially strong between Kade and me. Turning back, I stared at Violet, stunned by how different she looked. Her skin was no longer a pigmentless white, nope, now it was the shimmering pearly sheen that her wolf fur contained, almost like purple swirls of mecca were embedded in her skin, and everything about her glowed.

"You're glowing," I whispered. "So beautiful." My head swung to Kade, hands clutching at his shirt. "I can see the mecca. Is this what's it's like for both of you?"

Violet was the one to answer, a grin stretching across her face. "It's beautiful, isn't it?"

I could only nod, over and over, like a maniac. My brain was fried though. I could see the mecca and I had spoken with my biological mother. Only I wasn't sure how to process it all. Breathing deeply a few times, I finally released Kade's shirt and gripped his hand again.

"I'm ready. Let's send this energy back."

This time when I placed my hand on the stone and the portal opened to the Otherworld, these long thick purple lines burst out of the crystal. They shot in all different directions, and for some reason I could sense the thrums of mecca energy running along them. Concentrating as hard as I could, I sent my own energy through one of the lines. It zipped away, and I almost had a heart attack when it slammed up against something hard. Expanding out my magical vision, I was astonished to realize it was the mecca stone under the vortex of Queens.

A burst of understanding hit me, and with that came sparks of excitement. I knew exactly what to do now. Pulling my consciousness back to the room, I focused on the duller lines, those thinner and more fragile looking. These were the ties to the Otherworld, I was very sure. To double check, I let my energy zoom along one, and sure enough it smashed against a stone in one of the courts. Expanding my "vision" allowed me to glimpse a field of orange-leafed trees.

Fall Court.

I didn't know how long this new gift of seeing the mecca would last, if it was permanent or just a leftover from being inside the mecca with the Red Queen. I had to act quickly. Now that I knew where to send the extra overload of mecca, I gathered as much up as I could and *pushed*. At first it resisted me; the power wanted to stay right where it was. It had grown accustomed to the Earth side and did not want to go home.

Dragging up even more of my own strength, I not only physically pushed with my energy, but mentally I urged it to follow the mecca lines back to the other stones. As it started to funnel through the portal opening, it was like watching purple clouds being sucked through a vacuum, a magical storm rolling out.

My hair was whipping and flying around as the mecca clouds passed through me. Kade's muscles were shaking, I could feel them under my grip. No doubt it was taking everything he had to keep me from feeling the effects of channeling this much energy. Violet stepped into us; I felt her hand on my arm, and even more mecca rolled out through the lines. As the energy in the room lessened, it became easier to control the overflow, to see when the lines started to thicken and darken and look as vibrant as the Earth-side mecca. This was how I would know when to stop, to make sure we didn't give too much away. On the other side of the open portal, in the fae lands, the grass and the trees were now a bright vibrant green, the world again glowing with mecca. Healing.

Violet, Kade, and I had been funneling mecca for many minutes, and just when I was about to release the connection, the Red Queen's voice came floating through the mecca winds.

Enough.

That was the queen I remembered. I wrenched my hand up, hoping to remove it in one quick hit, but it seemed to be stuck.

"Kade!" I said, with some urgency, still trying to rip my hand off.

This was like being in the runaway car with no brakes again. I was ready now to get off the ride, but there was too much momentum. Violet let out a curse and shot a bolt of power into my arm. With a brief popping sound, I was thrown back, landing hard on the ground. The second I hit the floor my mecca sight vanished, as well as the portal. Kade knelt down beside me, taking deep breaths.

I put my hand on his face, noting his bloodshot eyes, beads of sweat coating his skin. "Are you okay?"

He nodded but didn't yet speak. Violet was the one to say, "If it wasn't for Kade's gift, we would have all been ripped in half."

Thank the gods my mate was not only brave and strong, but also fierce. He would never give up, not until there was no hope at all left.

Kade cleared his throat and I could see the broken capillaries in his eyes were already healing. "I know this is bad timing, but Selene is entering the palace. Nix said she's with ten guards and Sabina."

Dammit. She could have given me at least five minutes to pull myself together. Silver lining though – she wasn't out killing my people.

"We have the advantage," Kade said. "We know they're coming, so where do we want to take them on?"

I stood, my fatigue fading somewhat as focus washed over me. "The basement where Selene almost ended Finn's life. That's where I'll end hers."

Violet grinned. "Let's get your crown back."

We walked to the edge of the room and Finn loped to my side. I had kept up my end of the deal with the Summer Court and fixed the mecca. Now it was time to fight for my people. And if I failed, well, I could think of no greater way to die. Kade's strong hand slipped into mine and squeezed. *Not gonna happen.* His reassurance caressed my mind, the heat of his energy slipping inside of me, mingling with my own energy. Wolf and bear were stronger together. Selene would learn that very soon.

As we reached the doors out into the small library that hid the mecca room, voices could be heard out in the hall. I hurried over – Carrie was still out there, maybe trying to dissuade others from entering. She might need our help, and we had promised not to leave her behind.

Kade and I drew our weapons and slowly opened the double doors. There was no time to waste. Not only did we need to help Carrie, we also needed to get down to the basement. The second the doors opened, I leapt forward, blade ready for action. Carrie and four male guards were standing about four feet from the entrance. Kade's warmth pressed into my back as the five turned to face us. They all bowed.

"Your Highness. We will fight for you," one of them said.

I let the sword fall to rest at my side, and smiled at each of them.

"Thank you. I appreciate your support." I was already striding forward, Finn, Violet, and Kade at my back. "We need to get to the basement right now. Selene is coming, and I intend on taking the crown from her and stopping this useless war before anyone gets hurt."

They fell into line, at the back of our group. No one said anything more as we entered a darkened stairwell and rushed down the many floors to the basement. Inside the two thousand square foot area, there were a total of four entries. I placed a guard on each one. Violet and Finn took point on one side. Kade and I protected the other.

Tightening my grip on my sword, I prepared myself for the fight to come. I would need to be quick. Selene might be bringing ten soldiers now, but she could have over a hundred here in minutes if she put a call out. I needed to take Calista's advice, play off her ego, and make her fight me one on one. Suddenly Kade grinned beside me, his fierce expression softening. Unusual enough that I had to ask: "What's so funny?"

"Nix just pecked Larak's eyes out. He's blind."

My grin matched his. Nix was getting a big fat juicy strip of meat from me later. Good girl.

Not sixty seconds passed before I heard Selene's shrill scream. "Arianna!"

I gripped my sword so tight my knuckles were white.

Bring it, bitch. I'm ready for you.

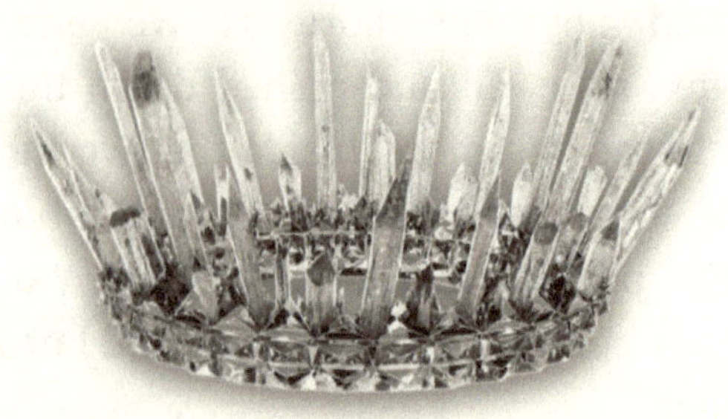

Chapter Fifteen

The blood of thy enemies is the liquid of thy victory.

THE DOUBLE DOORS to the entrance closest to me blasted open, knocking my guards off their feet. Sabina stepped in with Selene at her side, and ten guards funneled in behind them. Selene let out a shriek as she moved forward with a surge of mecca energy, and even though I hadn't been able to see the waves since releasing it back into the Otherworld, I felt more attuned to the magic of it. I could feel how much she was channeling.

She was dressed all in black – it actually looked like she was wearing a leather cat-suit, covered in armor and with pockets across her thighs. Probably where all her weapons were.

"You're dead, Arianna," she screamed, her face bright red, a series of red marks down her cheeks, like she had been clawing at her face. "For Larak I'm going to torture you slowly."

I remained calm as she stalked toward me with a hissing, blinded Larak across her shoulders, blood dripping from his eyes, his massive head swinging left and right frantically.

A sliver of sympathy for the animal pierced through me. He might be evil and slimy, but maybe that was Selene's influence. I mean, Finn was definitely his own being, good with no help from me, so probably Larak was as evil as his bonded heir. It was this thought that helped me shelve my weakness and harden my resolve.

To my right there was a heavy thud as Violet and Sabina crashed into each other, sparks of mecca flying around the arena. Their battle was hard and fast as they used a combination of physical and magical warfare. The ten guards followed Selene, who was still moving toward me.

I smirked, acting relaxed. "What's the matter, Selene? Afraid to fight me one on one?" She wanted to see my fear, and I would give her no such satisfaction. She didn't scare me. I was more than ready to take her down.

Selene's eyes practically glowed, and a purple sheen licked along her skin. She wore mecca like a coat. "That's *Your Highness*, not Selene. And I have every intention of killing you myself ... fae." She sneered the last part; the subtle changes to me had not escaped her attention. Turning to her guards, she shouted, "Kill the bear king!"

I tried to tamp down my fear. Even with ten highly trained guards, my mate could take care of himself, and I needed to focus.

"Kill her quickly, my love," Kade whispered, and then charged forward, sword raised to take on the line of guards. I was surprised to see that some of Selene's inner circle were not present. In fact, it looked like she was down more than a couple of guards. Had they defected from her? Another weakness for me to exploit, possibly. A queen was always going to be powerful, we had the power of our people within us, but as more defected from Selene, the less power she could wield.

The cat-suit clad shifter glided toward me, her eyes spitting with unbridled rage. Larak slid down to the ground, hissing as he slithered across the floor. His eyes were gone, but he still had strong senses and could scent where we were. I expected him to come straight for me, but he went for Finn.

My worry for my familiar was put on hold as Selene let out a shrieking battle cry, swinging her sword for my neck. Her attack was wild and uncontrolled, careless; she was full of emotion and weakness. I easily stepped aside, swiping her blade away with my own. Her emotions were going to be her downfall. I would make sure of it.

"What's really made you so mad, Selene?" I deflected another blow and kicked out, snapping her knee. She groaned and limped backward. "Is it that even though you did everything in your power to steal the crown from me, our people still prefer me? That deep down you know I will always be a better leader than you? That our people love me the most...?"

Selene's exotic features crumbled, her brows drawing together as red tinged her cheeks. She cried out in anger again, but this time she lunged and tried to take a swipe at Finn, who was close by, circling Larak. *Oh hell no.* Finn must have seen Selene coming. He rolled at the last second as a growl ripped from my throat. My familiar went back to Larak, keeping the snake in his focus. The serpent hadn't made any attempt to attack yet; losing his eyes had made him hesitant, but even without vision he was still deadly. Finn would not underestimate the creature.

Selene focused on me again. "The love of our people has made you weak. The Red Queen would be disgusted!" She lashed out with mecca, pushing me back a foot.

Her taunts brushed off me without even a twinge of hurt. I knew something she didn't – the Red Queen was anything but disgusted with me. She had protected me, to the point it had cost her her life.

I was getting tired of looking at Selene. I gathered up all of my magic, both mecca and fae, and pushed it right at her chest, adding a little extra width to include Larak.

Both she and her snake flew backward and slammed into the wall, and I kept my magic pressed into her, pinning them there.

"Help me, you idiots!" she shouted at her guards, but one quick glance over my shoulder told me that Kade, Carrie, and the other wolves who had joined our team, were having no problem keeping Selene's guards from reaching me. In fact, most of them were unconscious on the ground and of no use at all to Selene.

I felt her draw on the power of the mecca then, on the power of the people. It sparked something inside of me because I still held a bond to the shifters. My queen connection had never been properly severed. Selene started to fight back against my hold then, she was off the wall, stepping toward me. My legs shook as I continued pushing power at her, unsure if I would have enough juice to go against her now.

Selene grinned, and took another step closer. "I'm the true queen," she said, pride brimming in her tone. "The shifters give their power to me."

Everything inside of me rebelled at that statement. She was not a true queen, she was a thief. But there was something in what she said ... it reminded me of Bianca's statement. The Boston alpha had said that the defectors chose me, that they stood behind me. Which might mean I could use the same connection as Selene, I could still win this.

With unwavering faith in my people I sent out a call along the tattered queen bond still flickering within me. I called for the energy which would help me take Selene down. As the first burn of power hit my center, the redhead shifter let out a cry and fell to her knees. In a single burst of energy, the fae and mecca inside of me burned hot and bright, on the edge of being too much for me to handle. I felt all the shifters then, as I had when I was queen. Their love and energy. Their support.

It gave me the strength I needed to hold Selene in place. She was slumped forward on her knees, her face streaked with tears, black makeup running along her cheeks. Hardening my heart I stepped closer, ready to end this. I was done with Selene. This woman had stolen my crown, allowed hundreds of my people to be killed on the Island while she created a magical blanket, and worst of all, she had tried to kill my familiar. She had barely been queen for a week and was already trying to start a war between wolf and bear after years of peace – a peace that even the Red Queen had suffered to maintain.

Selene deserved death. Before I could reach her Larak's head shifted in my general direction; he hissed and lunged wildly at me. But he was slow, and had bad aim with his blindness. I was able to catch him easily, squeezing his head in my hands. Selene was fighting me again now, sobbing and shouting, "I'm the true queen, you are scum. I'll kill you and re-earn the love of the shifters." Her desperation was visible.

Making a split-second decision I pinched Larak's jaws so his teeth were bared, then taking a leap toward Selene, slammed his venom-filled fangs into her neck.

"Nooo!" she shouted at the same time Larak hissed.

Tightening my grip on the snake, I ripped him away from her and tossed him back to my waiting familiar. Finn wanted the honor of ending Larak's life. I would keep my eye on Selene. Pearlescent venom dripped slowly from the gaping holes in her neck, and as I heard the crunching of Finn taking Larak's head off behind me, Selene roared in agony.

I wanted revenge, but I wasn't evil. I didn't want Selene to feel the death of her familiar for too long. I lowered my head close to hers, and in a low voice, without inflection, I said, "You will die a failed queen. May you have more honor in your next life." She was beyond caring at this point. The death of her familiar had left her no more than a shell.

I dropped my hold on her at the same time I slashed my sword across her neck, taking her head clean off. Purple mecca blasted from her as her body crumpled to the floor.

I spun around to make sure the rest of my people were okay. Kade and Carrie were cutting down the last guards. Finn was standing beside Larak's headless body. And Violet – oh God, where was Violet? Sabina looked dead in the corner, but my best friend...

"Violet!" I shrieked frantically.

She appeared right before me, scaring the crap out of me. I grabbed my chest.

"Vi! You scared me."

She gave me a wink. "I wasn't going to walk over here through all that blood and ruin my new shoes."

I pulled her in for a hug, not even caring that she didn't like to be touched. I needed to feel her warmth, hear her heartbeat. I never wanted her taken from me again.

She squeezed me hard, then pulled back, looking me in the eyes. "Long live the queen!" she called over her shoulder.

Carrie, the two remaining guards, and Kade all bowed in agreement.

"What is your first order of business, My Queen?" Kade's deep voice carried across to me and I couldn't help but smile.

"Let's go stop this war. It's time to bring our people together. We've fixed the mecca and can live in peace once again." The shifters would have immediately felt the death of Selene, but since I still held a connection to the mecca and my people within me, there wouldn't be the usual backlash of power. The loss of control would be minimized.

Violet brushed her hands along her dress, wiping it clean of the debris she'd picked up fighting Sabina. "First we have to officially get your crown back. Which means you need to call a meeting of the packs."

She was right. Calista would be able to help me with that. She had contacts everywhere, she'd get word out.

"I want wolves and bears, together. We'll meet on the Island, and form an alliance tomorrow." A grin ripped across my tense features. "The council is about to find out what happens to shifters who betray me."

I hadn't slept in almost forty-eight hours, or longer, my last night's sleep being in the Otherworld before I was jailed. I took a brief nap on the boat across to the Island, but it was barely enough to keep me going. Calista and Gerald had very quickly gotten word out about the end of the war and called a meeting of the packs. Tomorrow morning I would go before all of my people. Not just my people, but also Kade's.

It was bad timing, having to wait another day to reclaim my crown – officially anyway. Selene had only been dead for a few hours, and already a slight weakness was spreading in our packs. As I predicted my queen bond was keeping it at bay, but we still had to sort this out immediately.

"Will they all make it in time?" Carrie asked me as the boat started to dock.

"Some will have to travel all night, but they'll make it," I said as I stood, widening my stance to keep my balance. "Calista has already spread our story, the evidence of what Selene was doing with Sabina, the way they allowed the fae to enter the night of the summer festival, the way the council betrayed all of us with their secrets and lies…" I stepped into Kade's heat, letting his body soothe my rough edges. "That this war with the bears is completely one-sided, and that bears and wolves are meant to rule together."

Kade's chest rumbled behind me. "Tomorrow morning we will petition to be co-rulers of the shifters, uniting our energy and the boroughs' mecca. Here's hoping they don't fight us too hard."

Our luck had never worked out that way, but it wouldn't matter. Somehow or other, I would make them see this was the new future for all of us.

As soon as we were off the boat, Violet, Carrie, Kade and I took an ATV to the bear estate. Even though I could have safely gone to the wolf estate, I needed to see my sister first. I was tense the entire drive, hands clutching on the sidebars. No one spoke. Kade was driving, expertly weaving in and out of the natural landscape. Finn was running; he needed to work off some energy. Nix was in the sky, keeping an eye out. Having a bird's eye view was turning out to be hugely useful. I wasn't sure how I'd lived before Kade and Nix.

"Winnie is fine," Kade said as he placed his hand across my thigh, which I was bouncing up and down. "Nix is already near the estate. She can see her playing in the garden."

A surge of relief and joy burst through me. I laced my fingers in Kade's and pulled our joined hands up close to my chest, cradling them. "I'm failing her as a mother slash sister. I keep promising myself I'll do better, and she keeps getting pushed aside for this crazy life I'm living. I don't want to be like that anymore. I don't want her to always be second."

Kade's grip tightened and our ATV ground to a halt as he turned to face me fully. "We will do better by Winnie." His voice was serious, no room for doubts. "We're going to be a family. She'll live with us, and we'll be there every single day for her. She'll never doubt that she's loved and wanted and protected. She's my cub now, and I'll not let either of you down."

I couldn't move or react, trembling in a way I had never experienced before. I knew I was going to crumble apart, but I desperately fought to keep myself together. It took me some time, but I regained control of my emotions. I threw myself into him, hugging him tightly for being so perfect, for loving me so much he was the glue to all my broken pieces. For also loving the most precious person in the world to me. Winnie.

When I pulled back, my voice was hoarse as I said, "Let's go get our cub."

From the corner of my eye I could see Carrie's huge smile and Violet's tear-streaked face, and a small part of my heart ached. I reached back and brushed my hand against Violets, ignoring her usual flinch as our energies collided. I then blew her a kiss, telling her silently that she was also my family, that I would always be there for her, and now she had Kade too. I might not have had the best experience with family, but that was going to change now. My version of a family would stick together. We would have each other's backs. We would stand against all who tried to tear us apart.

Exiting the ATV, I sprinted into the garden, following the sounds of childish laughter. My heart was beating rapidly as Winnie came into sight, her hair a mess of waves, her cheeks pink. She didn't see me until I was almost on top of her; her eyes lit up as I dashed up and scooped her into my arms.

"Sissy!" she shrieked in my ear. Fat, hot tears were already dripping down my cheeks as I stood there holding her, trying my best not to squeeze the life out of her in my need to be close to her.

Wiggling her way back a little, she placed a tiny hand on my cheek, her eyes serious and looking far older than her five years. "Why are you crying, Ari? I missed you so much. Don't cry. I'll look after you."

The dam burst and actual sobs escaped from my tightly pressed lips. Winnie wound her arms around my neck then and hugged me hard. She *was* looking after me in the innocent way of a child.

"I love you so much, Win. I love you more than anything else in this world. More than any crown or title."

She pulled back again and patted my cheek this time. "I know you do, silly. You always say you love me." She quieted a moment. "Will you have to go away again? I don't like it when you leave."

I shook my head a few times, a frantic back and forth, before I calmed enough to say, "I promise you, Win, I am going to do everything in my power to ensure we're not apart like that anymore. Kade and I are going to try and rule together. You'll live with us. You're our family and we are sticking together."

She looked thoughtful as she asked: "Like having real parents?"

More sobs were trying to emerge, but I kept them contained. "Yes, baby girl, exactly like having real parents. We'll never let anyone hurt you. You'll be safe and loved every single day."

Kade, who had been hovering close by, stepped into us now and wrapped his long arms around us both. His warmth and energy was everywhere, and I let him hold me up, because my legs were so weak. Winnie giggled, popping her head up and brushing her lips across my cheek and then Kade's. "I think I'm going to like having parents." Then she wiggled and I knew it was time to let her go. Five year olds only have so much hug threshold before they need their freedom.

When she was back on her bare feet, her little head darted around. "Can you help me find Chase? He's hiding somewhere and I have been looking forever!"

I turned to Kade and he grinned. "Chase is my nephew."

Winnie bobbed her head up and down. "Yes, he's my best friend. We play every day and we're going to be mermaids and pirates when we grow up."

I bent so my head was level with hers and gave her a bright grin. "Glad you found that bear best friend you've been looking for, Win. Now … let's see if we can find that sneaky cub."

She let out a delighted shriek and then we were off, running through Kade's luscious garden, playing hide and seek. In a few hours' time I'd have to rest and prepare for tomorrow, but for now there was nothing else in the world I'd rather be doing. Even though exhaustion was beckoning for me to sleep, and Kade as well, we played in the garden for over two hours, running after Chase and Winnie, making animals noises and hiding behind trees. It was finally around 3

P.M that I lost my battle with my heavy eyes and my head began to dip down into my half-eaten sandwich.

"Ari needs a nap!" Winnie giggled, which had Chase bursting into fits of laughter.

Looking at sweet Winnie now, something hit me, hard. She wasn't my sister, not biologically. Different mom and dad. She felt more like a daughter. Might as well be. Calista and I had raised her since she was a day old. It made me love and cherish her more.

Reaching over, I squeezed her little hand. "I think I do need a nap. Will you be okay?" If she begged me to stay awake and play more, I would.

Winnie waved a hand at me. "I'm fine! Chase and I are going to find the mermaid cove and steal all of the pirate treasures there."

I nodded. "Okay, as long as mermaid cove is in this backyard?"

One of Winnie's attendants nodded, and I smiled. Kade had been watching me, beneath heavy lidded eyes of his own, and now he stood, taking my hand. Without another word we crossed into the house and walked down the hall to the bedroom. Once inside, I kicked off my shoes, belt, and slid my bra from beneath my shirt. Screw showering, screw pj's, screw sex, I just wanted sleep. I fell into the thick feather-topped mattress and a sigh escaped my lips.

Kade sat perched on the edge of the bed. He let out a low, deep chuckle. "Sometimes I'm not sure if you love me or sleep more."

I smiled. "It's a tie, really."

He wasn't undressing or lying beside me.

Leaning over, he kissed my cheek. "I'll be back in an hour to sleep beside you. I need to see my mother about something."

"Mmmkay," I mumbled, and that's when the exhaustion took me.

I awoke to early morning light on my face. You know that feeling you get after an incredibly satisfying night's sleep, that full body relaxation? I had that, and no wonder. One look at the alarm clock on the dresser told me I'd slept for fifteen hours. I rolled over and took in the sight of my big bear, his long body stretched out at my side, chest rising and falling. He actually looked pretty peaceful for Kade. Normally he had all of this energy and strength just naturally exuding from his body.

I decided to have a quick shower and then see if he was awake. I crept from the bed and entered his massive bathroom. While showering, I ran over a hundred different scenarios in my head about what I would say to my people today, needing the right words to make them understand everything that had been happening lately. Not to mention the changes in me now. I was going to have to go out there and speak of an enemy that most of them would never have heard of, the fae, and in the same breath tell them I was half one.

By the time I had brushed my teeth and dressed, I still wasn't sure what I could say that would sway them to see my side of things. In the end, it would come down to majority rule. Not everyone would be happy with bears and wolves ruling side by side, or with me being part fae, but hopefully enough would see the benefits of having me return as queen. In time, everyone would see that it could work.

I was so lost in my thoughts that when I opened the bathroom door that led into the adjoining master bedroom, I slammed into Kade. He was shirtless, with wet hair.

"Sorry." I placed my hands on his chest and let them brush over his abdomen. "Where did you shower?"

His eyes were dark as they ran across my face. "I used a guest bathroom."

I let my hands trail the elastic of his boxers. "You could have joined me."

His eyes lightened to a brilliant copper. "I decided to give you a little time alone. I know you're nervous about the speech today. Plus, I had some things to think about too."

My hand froze. I didn't like it when my normally unflappable bear got that slightly uneasy look on his face. "Is everything okay? Anything I can help you with?"

One of Kade's hands had been slack at his side, and he pulled it up between us now, opening his palm to show a beautiful diamond ring. The stone was large and oval, with a multitude of smaller diamonds running along the side and down the band. My breath caught in my throat. "I want to give you all the time you need. We can have a long engagement, but I've wanted to ask you this for so long ... I refuse to wait any longer. I had an elaborate thing planned, lots of surprises, but that's just not you." He knew me so well. Simple and private was what I liked. He leaned down and pressed his lips to mine, pulling back just long enough to say, "Arianna, will you marry me?"

Once I was able to process all of the beautiful emotions running through me, I used our bond to reply, *Yes.*

He grinned, slipping the ring on my finger. It was a perfect fit.

"It was my grandmother's," Kade said as he stroked my hand.

"It's beautiful," I replied breathlessly. It was perfect.

I would go into this meeting fully committed to a bear and wolf partnership. Kade's lips crashed into mine and all thoughts of a meeting were swept from my mind. Actually, all thoughts of anything other than the feel and scent of my mate were gone.

Kade lifted me into his arms, and my legs did their usual wrap-around-him thing. In a flash he had moved us out of the bathroom and my back was against the wall, Kade pressing into me. My mouth opened as his tongue danced with mine; our kisses soon turning hot and heavy. Kade peppered kisses down my jaw, before trailing them further down.

"We don't have long," Kade said against my skin.

My head went back as he hit the sensitive spot behind my ear. "I won't need long," I said with a laugh-groan.

His chest rumbled, and I knew his bear was happy. I was happy too. We had just enough time to celebrate our new journey together, and then we would go see our people, and fight for our continued existence.

After breakfast, it was time to head to the meeting spot. Kade, Violet, and I were waiting and ready. Monica, Blaine, and Victor would be our guard. My nerves had settled down slightly. I would accept whatever outcome was handed down today. I would survive either way. I had Kade, Winnie, and the rest of my family. If the wolves decided this was not a road for them, I would be with the bears. They were my people now too.

Seriously though, I was engaged to a bear, had killed Selene, and was about to try to unite two races after hundreds of years at war. At this point, not much could shock me. Or so I thought until I stepped out onto the front porch and a sleek black sedan pulled up. Two people stepped out that I hadn't expected to see and I literally gasped, almost tripping down the stairs.

It wasn't Calista's presence per se that shocked me, though I had expected her to stay and care for Baladar. It was Baladar himself, on the Island, not a prisoner in his loft, that left me open-mouthed.

"Of course!" Violet shouted, running to greet Baladar. She didn't touch him, which was normal, but she got right up in his face. Kade and I remained on the porch, both of us trying to figure out what had happened.

"When I killed Sabina the spell broke, didn't it?" Violet was looking like a student asking her teacher if she got a hundred percent on her quiz.

Baladar winked at Violet and nodded. That was when I realized the light blue coloring of his iris had returned. It also seemed, by the way he looked right at Violet, that he could see her.

I hurried down the stairs to them now. "You're not blind." My voice was high with happiness, which only increased as I noticed Calista's and Baladar's hands intertwined. "This is such wonderful news! I'm so very happy for you." My gaze found my advisor, who looked radiantly happy. "For both of you."

Baladar nodded, pulling his love closer to him. "For the first time in over a century I'm tasting freedom, and it's perfect." His eyes locked in on me. "I'm here now to help, to repay some of the debt I owe you."

My eyes caught on the shine of my diamond, and I felt the strength of my mate through our bond. "I have everything I need. You owe me nothing."

Reaching into the sedan, Baladar pulled out an old brown leather book. He handed it to me. Frowning, I gently cracked the spine, glancing across the first few pages. There were old black and white photographs with names and dates, like a family tree. But as I read further, I gasped. Baladar had given me a royal family tree for bear and wolf shifter married couples.

"Bears and wolves were always meant to rule side by side. Make them see that," Baladar said, and I nodded, handing the book to Violet.

"Thank you." I pressed my hand to my chest, trying to keep my emotions in check. We were going to bring our case to the people. We were going to make them see. Bears and wolves were stronger together.

Chapter Sixteen

Long live the queen.

ALPHAS, PACK MEMBERS, and even lone shifters had come from all around the world. Bears and wolves together. Tens of thousands of them filled the Island. I had seriously underestimated Calista's ability to get word out in a very short period of time.

We were set up on the same hill where the mid-summer festival and stage had been. At first Calista protested, saying there were too many raw memories of those we had lost there, but I wanted them to understand what was at stake here, that those losses were nothing compared to what we could sustain if we didn't join together and lock the fae out of our world. Even though I had fixed the mecca, I knew the winter queen would not be satisfied. She wanted the earth side mecca and would stop at nothing to get it. She also wanted the power inside of me. I had no idea where or when they would hit, but we needed to be prepared for her attack.

I stood on the edge of the huge platform, thousands of shifters spread out before me, bears along the left side, wolves on the right. Unlike last time, there was a decent gap separating the two races down the center. Selene had done this. In her very short time screwing up the role of queen, she had someone managed to increase the already too large divide between our people.

"You ready, Ari?" Kade was at my side and Finn by my legs, but I would step out alone.

The wolf council were not in sight yet, but I knew they were out there, lingering in the outer areas. They would jump in if I failed, to try and wrest control of the wolves from me. I couldn't let that happen. They would continue down the same path as Selene.

Straightening my shoulders, I smoothed down my red silk dress. Calista had gone all out with my appearance. My hair was pinned up in a braid crown. I wore my arm cuffs, and had my sword strapped across my back. The sheath was from Kade's armory, and I might have shed a few tears thinking of how Ben wasn't here to find me the right piece. Actually, standing here, all the memories of my friend came flooding up from the box I had shoved them into, the box in which I had stored all my grief because there had been no room, no time for it. This still wasn't the time, but my emotions were dangerously close to the surface, especially when I caught sight of Victor and Blaine – rigid jaws, hard eyes, throats working. They were close to losing it too, but they didn't. I drew strength from their strength, and I walked out onto the stage.

A large group to my right let out a cheer as I moved across the platform. I turned to find Bianca front and center; behind her were hundreds of wolf shifters, many of them I recognized as the defectors who had been at Kade's Staten Island mansion. They wore proud expressions, their warmth and energy touching my heart and bringing a true smile to my face. I inclined my head toward the shifters who had helped me destroy Selene, before turning back to the larger crowd. I was center stage now, staring out across a sea of shifters.

There had been a lot of noise until this point: arguing, fighting, crying over lost loved ones, even some laughter. For many this was a reunion. But as I stood alone, facing out toward them, a hushed silence slowly descended over the hill. I didn't speak straight away, I let the silence reign until there was only the birds, the ocean, the thousands of heartbeats in the clearing.

It was clear that my fae-ness had shocked them, but so far no one was screaming obscenities at me. Taking this as a good sign, I used the mecca to project my voice far out into the clearing.

"Thank you all for coming today on such short notice. Thank you for giving me a chance to explain to you everything that has happened over the past few months."

A few whispers echoed around, but for the most part I could tell I had their attention. "I want to start our new relationship with the truth. I won't hide things from you like the council and previous leaders have." Gasps and curses rang out. "They told us that wolves and bears were enemies. That the bears would destroy us. That we should attack first. This was a LIE!"

I added more mecca because they were starting to get louder. "In the beginning, bears and wolves ruled together."

This caused the most uproar. Turning my head, I gave Violet a nod, and she lifted the book from Baladar up in her hands, and then with a blast of energy the information on the pages projected above the crowd as if on a movie screen, ten feet tall so everyone could see.

"This is the first family tree," I told the hushed crowd. "Bears and wolves are opposites in lots of ways for a reason. Male heirs for the bears, female for the wolves. This is because our true mates lie within the other races. King Kade is my bonded mate." Another series of loud cries from the crowd. I could sense their disbelief, and maybe even slivers of hope. "He is my true bonded mate. We are connected and have a mental link."

As I spoke Violet continued flicking through the pages, through the history, through the family trees. Kade stepped up at my side and linked his hand through mine. He wore his golden crown, and had on his royal armor, full military style. He had never been more beautiful, and I found myself growing even more confident standing with him.

I lifted our joined hands. "Together Kade and I can control the mecca in a way no other can." We gave a quick demonstration, shooting out blasts of energy, sharing it with all of our shifters. "Together our people can fight the true enemy who has caused all the mayhem and destruction in our world over the past few months. The fae."

"You're one of them! Why should we trust you?" This cry came from the other side of the stage, and I wasn't even remotely surprised to find the wolf council standing there. Well, most of them anyway. I could see eight or nine members.

It was Torin who had spoken. "You come back here looking exactly like the Tuatha, and you kill our queen. Why should anyone believe a lying, treasonous, snake like you, Arianna. You are just like your aunt, a failed queen. A traitor. A disgrace."

Rage ripped through me and I lashed out at Torin with fae power, forcing him to kneel. Everyone gasped and backed up a few paces, staring at the kneeling councilman.

Looking up, I spoke to my people, laying my fragile soul bare for all to see. "I am a victim of lies as well. I found out only a few days ago that my true mother was the Red Queen herself, and..." I struggled to finish, tears lining my eyes, but I swallowed them down and said. "My biological father was fae, a very evil fae who I hope to kill. I didn't know any of this until I went to the Otherworld to get Violet back."

Silence washed over the crowd, and these weird looks of pity and respect began to roll in. I hated their pity, but I was empowered by the clear evidence that I was reaching them. Some of them anyway.

"Selene robbed me of my crown without proper evidence, started a needless war between the wolves and the bears ... so yes, I killed her. Kade and I restored the mecca, which was the only shot we had to stop the fae from attacking. I don't want to rule again by force. I want a democracy. I want change. The ways of old are dead and I want a new stronger pack for all of us!" I roared and they roared right back.

I opened my arms. "I leave you with a choice. You can join Kade and I as we embark on this new adventure of having a bigger, stronger, combined pack. We'll open the borders to the five boroughs and share the mecca. I will be your queen and he your king, and you will all have a chance at finding your bonded mate." The crowd was deadly silent. "Or you can hold another Summit, choose from the next batch of heirs, and stick to your old ways. I will live in Staten Island with the bears and wish you nothing but love and good tidings."

I dropped my hands and let one hot tear fall down my cheek. I hoped they could feel the emotions I was projecting, how much I loved them, how much I wanted for my people to prosper and love and be happy. I felt them all inside of me, through the mecca, each beautiful soul.

Bianca made her move then, pushing through the crowd, making her way over to where I had Torin pinned on his knees. People were murmuring, talking about what they wanted to do, and I just stood there ready for any outcome they chose. The Boston alpha stood behind Torin and in a single swift move unsheathed her sword slicing it across the councilmembers throat. Torin fell forward, his blood flooding out in a rush.

The Boston alpha turned toward the crowd. "Long live Queen Arianna!"

Thousands of voices echoed her call and I lost it. Tears rolled down my cheeks as I heard the cries of my people. "Long live Queen Arianna! Long live King Kade!"

The majority were screaming. A few dozen wolf shifters began to walk away, the old council members with them. Good. Let them go. Leave New York City and never come back.

Kade wiped a tear from my cheek. "The people have spoken."

Violet crossed the stage, and in her hands was the wooden box that held my mecca crown. I had no idea how she had managed to retrieve that, and it was probably better not to know. Taking a deep breath, I opened the box and since I was the only one who could touch the mecca piece, I settled it on my head. The crowd went wild, and for the first time the wolves and bears began to mingle, shaking hands, introducing themselves, walking around to both sides. I had no misconceptions that this joining was going to be easy, but clearly enough people had been following the journey of me and Kade. They could hear the truth in what I said. They wanted change.

Kade, Violet, and I remained on stage. Calista and Baladar soon joined us. We were all smiling, and I was just about to call for celebrations when a popping came from behind me. I whirled around to see a portal opening. Baladar and Violet rushed in front of me, hands raised, ready to defend us. A single figure pitched forward from the swirling mass of energy, and I let out a cry when I saw Dalia slumped across the stage. An unnatural silence descended across the crowds behind me; no doubt all of them were waiting to see what had happened. Pushing my people out of the way I dropped down beside Dalia, who was not moving. I turned her, tears springing to my eyes at the sight of her stomach sliced open, too much blood seeping free.

"Someone heal her!" I screamed as I placed two hands over her bleeding abdomen. A snap of energy signaled that the portal was gone.

The fae's lips were worryingly pale as she tilted her head back to see the crown atop my head. A weak smile lit up her face, before a frown slowly replaced it. She leaned up a little, and whispered in my ear. "Darkness... and the Winter Court... coming for you."

I gave a sharp inhale of breath. Violet was there then, her healing energy flooding into the fae, but it was too late. Dalia gave one last shuddering breath, then her vibrant eyes turned dull and glassy.

Sorrow bloomed in my chest as I met my best friend's gaze. She looked both stunned and horrified as she tore her eyes from mine to glance back at Dalia. As I got to my feet, Kade's hand at my back, I realized the crowd was very noisy again.

Someone shouted out, "What did she say, Your Majesty? What happened?"

I moved to the edge of the stage, hands bloody, heartbroken. I had promised not to lie to my people anymore. "The Winter Court is coming. They have attacked our allies, but we will be ready for them. We will take them down and they will regret ever stepping foot in our boroughs!"

The swarm of shouts and screams filled the hill, echoing out into the ocean. In that moment, with Kade at my side, and my people out there before me, I almost believed we stood a chance.

***

Acknowledgements from Leia: As always thanks to my bestie Jaymin Eve for being such a fun creative writing partner. I have loved writing all of these books with you! A big thank you to Lela, my PA for putting up with my crazy on a daily basis. Thanks to my wonderful hubby and family for helping out around the house so I can write. Thank you to Lee our editor, my release team and beta's for all of your hard work to make sure this book was error free. Can't wait for you all to read the final installment. This series has been so fun. ❤

Acknowledgements from Jaymin: Thank you to Leia Stone, you're the best friend a girl could ask for. Thanks for making our "job" so much fun. To Heather, my PA, thank you for being amazing. Honestly, you go above and beyond for me, and I couldn't ask for a better friend. Don't ever leave me, because I'll find you. Sorry, that was a little creepy. But seriously, I will find you.

Thank you to Lee, our editor, and to Tamara, our amazing cover designer. Both of you are so important in bringing our creations to life and we are so grateful to you.

To my release team (and Nerd Herd) ... you are seriously some of my favourite people ever. Your encouragements, enthusiasm for the written word, not to mention help with edits and sharing on release day, means so much to me. I really lucked out with every single one of you. FYI - You also can't leave. It's written in an acknowledgements now, which means you are obligated to stay. Forever.

Lastly to my family. You are my everything. Therefore, I am nothing without you. Love you more than all the words in all the books.

Books from Jaymin Eve

A Walker Saga - YA Paranormal Romance series
(complete) Ages 13+
First World - #1
Spurn - #2
Crais - #3
Regali - #4
Nephilius - #5
Dronish - #6
Earth - #7

Supernatural Prison Trilogy - NA Urban Fantasy
series (complete) Ages 17+
Dragon Marked - #1
Dragon Mystics - #2
Dragon Mated - #3

Supernatural Prison Stories
Broken Compass - #1

Sinclair Stories Ages 18+ Contemporary Sports
Romance
Songbird - Standalone Contemporary Romance

Hive Trilogy Urban Fantasy
(Vampires)(Complete) Ages 15+
Ash - #1
Anarchy - #2

Annihilate: #3

<u>NYC Mecca Series Urban Fantasy Ages 15+</u>
Queen Heir
Queen Alpha
Queen Fae
Queen Mecca

<u>Curse of the Gods Series High Fantasy Reverse
Harem Series Ages 15-17+</u>
Trickery
Persuasion

Stay in touch with Jaymin:
www.facebook.com/JayminEve.Author
Mailing list: www.jaymineve.com
jaymineve@gmail.com